"It was private. Just between us."

"And you really expect me to believe that?" Porscha asked. "It's been three years, Xavier, and you've never tried to clear the air. So why now?"

"When I saw you upstairs on that television screen, I knew it wasn't over between us, Porscha." Xavier moved from the spot where he'd been rooted and strolled toward her. Porscha stepped backward until her hip hit the mirrored cabinet behind her. There was no place for her to run. "And seeing you up close and in person, I'm certain of it."

"You don't know what you're talking about."

He reached out and tunneled his hand through her hair, bringing her closer toward him. "I don't think so, but feel free to prove me wrong." He lowered his head, and when she was inches away from his face, he said, "Tell me you don't want this."

* * *

A Game Between Friends by Yahrah St. John is part of the Locketts of Tuxedo Park series.

Dear Reader,

I can't believe it's here. The final book in the Locketts of Tuxedo Park series and it has Xavier Lockett front and center. I loved that Xavier's been in the shadows during the last few books because it sets the stage for him to shine now.

When he meets beautiful songstress Porscha Childs at a therapy facility, she's weary of the pressures of fame and he's trying to accept losing his first love, football. They strike up a friendship that quickly turns to lust, but a misunderstanding forces them apart.

I loved this second-chance love story because the chemistry between Xavier and Porscha is undeniable and something neither is willing to give up. Watching the push and pull in their relationship is addictive and I hope you'll be equally caught up in their secret love affair as they hide from the media all while discovering love is worth fighting for.

Want more sexy and dramatic contemporary romances? Sign up for my newsletter at www.yahrahstjohn.com or contact me at yahrah@yahrahstjohn.com.

All the best,

Yahrah St. John

YAHRAH ST. JOHN

A GAME BETWEEN FRIENDS

HARLEQUIN
DESIRE

HARLEQUIN®
DESIRE™

ISBN-13: 978-1-335-73567-6

A Game Between Friends

Copyright © 2022 by Yahrah Yisrael

Recycling programs
for this product may
not exist in your area.

For questions and comments about the quality of this book, please contact us at CustomerService@Harlequin.com.

Harlequin Enterprises ULC
22 Adelaide St. West, 41st Floor
Toronto, Ontario M5H 4E3, Canada
www.Harlequin.com

Printed in U.S.A.

Yahrah St. John is the proud author of forty-one books with Harlequin Desire, Kimani Romance and Arabesque as well as her own indie works.

When she's not at home crafting one of her steamy romances with compelling heroes and feisty heroines with a dash of family drama, she is gourmet cooking or traveling the globe seeking out her next adventure. For more info, visit www.yahrahstjohn.com or find her on Facebook, Instagram, Twitter, BookBub or Goodreads.

Books by Yahrah St. John

Harlequin Desire

The Stewart Heirs

At the CEO's Pleasure
His Marriage Demand
Red Carpet Redemption

Locketts of Tuxedo Park

Consequences of Passion
Blind Date with the Spare Heir
Holiday Playbook
A Game Between Friends

Visit her Author Profile page at Harlequin.com, or yahrahstjohn.com, for more titles.

You can also find Yahrah St. John on Facebook, along with other Harlequin Desire authors, at Facebook.com/harlequindesireauthors!

To my mom, Asilee Mitchell,
for showing me what true courage looks like.

Prologue

"Darling, I'm thrilled you could join us this evening," Angelique Lockett gushed when her son Xavier arrived at the skybox lounge at the Atlanta Cougars stadium.

His older brothers, Roman and Julian, and sister, Giana, had already arrived to watch the game. His new sister-in-law, Shantel, was also there.

"Hey, Ma." Xavier approached his mother and kissed her cheek. She eyed his ensemble. He'd come casually dressed in dark jeans, Jordan sneakers and, in a nod to his mother, a button-down blue shirt.

His work schedule as a sportscaster usually didn't allow him to attend Sunday games during the football season, but the network wanted to test out a new weekend commentator, so Xavier was sitting this one out. And before taking this job, Xavier had never had much opportunity to enjoy the family's private skybox, with its plush beige carpet, upholstered chairs, mahogany-paneled walls holding large television screens, and the huge marble-encased bar. *That was* because he'd been on the football field. But that was another lifetime.

The knee injury he'd sustained three years ago when he'd been the Cougars quarterback ended any chance he'd ever have of playing ball again. Xavier felt like a failure. He'd let down his old man. Let the team down. Before he was injured, the Atlanta Cougars were on a winning streak and poised to win their first championship, but then Xavier had made a wrong move that landed him under a mountain of men. He'd been carried off the field on a stretcher. It had been demoralizing.

"Should I be concerned you're not on-air?" his father inquired. Josiah had used his connections to help Xavier get the job, but that wasn't why he'd kept it. Xavier excelled at everything he did and once he found his groove, sportscasting had been no different. "You know there's always a place in the coaching department of the Atlanta Cougars."

"Everything's fine," Xavier replied and came toward the bar where Julian was stationed, drinking a tumbler of dark liquid. It wasn't the first time his father had brought up the possibility of him coaching the team, and Xavier suspected it wouldn't be the last.

"You avoided the hot seat," Julian said with a grin. "Must be one of our turns."

Xavier grinned back. There was no love lost between Julian and their father. They were incompatible. "Sorry, bro."

Julian was a smooth talker, and the ladies loved his

toffee coloring, curly fade, light brown eyes and perpetual five-o'clock shadow. He was fashionably dressed in navy trousers and a silk shirt. He made Xavier his usual, a Scotch on the rocks, which he accepted. Xavier took a generous swallow to take the edge off—being here at the stadium was never easy. Brought back too many memories.

"The game should be starting soon," his mother announced. "I'll have the staff bring around the canapés."

Xavier and Julian both chuckled. Usually, they ate football fare when watching a game, like wings, nachos, bratwurst or chips and dip, but if their mother was in attendance? Only elevated appetizers would do.

"What are you two whispering about?" Giana asked, coming toward them. His beautiful, chocolate-hued sister wore a jean jumpsuit with a large belt wrapped around her slender waist. She wasn't quite as tall as Xavier, but she was statuesque and reached his shoulders. Her ebony hair was the same as their mother's, except Giana wore hers with wispy bangs.

"Staying off Dad's radar," Julian responded.

"Good luck with that." Giana chuckled.

"You better hope he doesn't ask you about Wynn Starks and why you haven't secured a sports drink endorsement contract with him yet," Julian quipped.

Giana rolled her eyes. "Don't you worry about a thing. I always get my man." She gave him a wink.

Their attention turned to the ninety-two-inch television screen. The game hadn't started, but the commentators were talking about the odds of the Atlanta Cougars winning, now that they had a new quarterback in Wayne Brown.

"Darn straight," Josiah shouted from across the room. "He's a terrific addition to the team and will get us a championship."

Is that a dig at me? Xavier wondered.

A light had gone out in Josiah's eyes when the doctors told Xavier he would never play football again. Xavier didn't know who was more upset, he or his father. So he'd allowed Josiah to bring in doctor after doctor, specialist after specialist until eventually Xavier had told him to stop. He was never going to be fixed.

Did that also mean he wasn't good enough to be Josiah's son?

It had taken Xavier months in therapy to realize he couldn't let football define him. The counselor had helped him see his life was his own and he could and *should* make choices that made *him* happy. Instead, as soon as he returned to Atlanta from the clinic, his father had pushed his agenda. Become a sports commentator, he'd said. And being the dutiful son, Xavier had complied.

"You're awfully quiet," Giana said from his side. "Are you okay?"

Xavier sipped his drink. "Sure."

She eyed him suspiciously. "I don't believe that for a second."

Xavier shrugged and focused his attention on the television screen because he couldn't believe his eyes. Standing in the middle of the field was Porscha Childs. Xavier blinked several times to be sure he wasn't hallucinating.

He wasn't.

Damn, she still looked good.

No, correct that. She looked *better*.

The years had been kind to her. The singer's tawny-brown skin gleamed. Her deep-set light brown eyes sparkled while her long jet-black hair hung in tussled waves down her slender back. She was smoking hot in a royal blue tuxedo dress with a deep V neckline. Her lush lips were bright red and totally kissable.

It made Xavier recall another time when he'd gotten to taste Porscha's lips.

Xavier had been at a wellness facility in Colorado that specialized in care for the mind and body. The facility was frequented by athletes and celebrities, so Xavier had signed up to attend and rehabilitate his knee but also work on his mental health. Losing his lifelong dream had resulted in a deep depression.

Before arriving at the clinic, he'd wallowed for months until his father gave him a kick in the butt and told him to work out his issues. It was exactly what Xavier needed to jump-start him on the road to recovery. And so he'd flown to the facility in Colorado, and every day he dutifully worked the program, physical therapy in the mornings and group therapy in the afternoons.

It was there that he met the most stunning creature he'd ever seen. The first time he saw her, she was trying her best to be unassuming in a large kimono sweater wrapped around her frame. Her long black hair hung in a ponytail down her back, but it was her light brown eyes that spoke to him. Maybe because it was clear she didn't want to be there. She looked terrified of being called on by the group leader, who was known for putting newbies on the spot to get them to talk. It hadn't been easy for Xavier, either, to explain to the group why he was in therapy, but he'd done it, and she would, too.

He'd moved toward her and as he approached, her eyes landed on him. Xavier took a seat beside her. "Hey, name's Xavier."

Her eyes had drifted downward, and he'd wondered if she was going to speak, but then she'd said, "Hi."

"Is that all I get? I told you my name." He'd offered her a smile.

When she glanced up at him, he'd groaned and squeezed his eyes shut for a split second before opening them again. Heavens! Up close, her eyes were designed to make a man melt. She'd given him a half smile and his eyes zoomed to her delicious mouth, which had a tint of pink lipstick. "I'm Porscha." She'd held out her small hand.

Xavier took it in his and shook it. He'd been ready to say they could be friends during their stay, but something told him he and Porscha were going to be more than friends. *Much more.*

"She's amazing, isn't she?" Giana said from Xavier's side, bringing him back to the present as Porscha belted out the national anthem. "I love all her music."

"Yeah, she's all right," Julian commented from behind them. "I don't know if I could handle all the attention that comes with being with someone as famous as her."

"You get plenty of press," Xavier responded, defending Porscha.

Julian shrugged. "Local stuff. But her—" he pointed to the television "—the national press dogs her. That's a lot of pressure to live up to."

They had no idea, Xavier thought.

He recalled his and Porscha's discussion in the clinic about how she was always trying to keep up with her public persona and how when she failed, the public were quick to criticize. It was hard living up to the idealized version they had in their mind of who and what she should be.

He missed Porscha.

They'd been good together *in* and *out* of bed.

Maybe he could do something about that.

Xavier placed his drink on the bar. "I'll be right back." He knew his family would probably think he needed a break because of the game. He tended to avoid the stadium, but that wasn't it. He had to see Porscha.

"Where are you going?" his father asked. "The game is about to start."

"I'll be back," Xavier murmured and quickly left the skybox. Once in the corridor, he raced toward the elevator that would take him to the lower level. He was betting Porscha wouldn't immediately leave the stadium but would instead go back to the dressing room and grab her things before escaping.

Xavier hoped he wasn't wrong.

Porscha was exhausted. She'd taken a red-eye from Germany, where she'd held a concert the night before at a military base. All she wanted was to go home, curl up in her own bed and go to sleep. Instead, her mother and manager, Diane Childs, had insisted she take this last-minute request to sing the national anthem for the Atlanta Cougars after another songstress bowed out due to a bout of laryngitis.

"The next six months are crucial," Diane had said once they were in the dressing room after last night's performance. "It's the final stretch before the Grammys. We want to keep your name on everyone's lips. The more exposure for you, the better."

And Porscha had relented.

She had worked too hard to get to this point. She had come from nothing. Her mother had gotten pregnant at eighteen and married her father, who'd eventually left them in relative poverty for another woman, whom he married and started another family with. Her mother had been devastated and consequently put all her focus on Porscha. When she had discovered Porscha could sing, she put her in singing competitions. Eventually, Porscha was picked up by a small record label.

Her first album had been a multiplatinum success, garnering her three Grammys and countless awards from Billboard to American Music. But success had brought its own scrutiny. The press were tough because she wasn't the average model size. Porscha thought the world was her oyster and then the second album came, bringing with it the sophomore jinx. *It bombed.* The press had been critical, and she'd fallen off the pedestal.

Afterward, she'd tumbled into a vicious depression, which only became worse when her father died a short while later. Although he'd contributed financially, she hadn't had a relationship with him prior to his passing, so his death, and the fact she would never get a resolution to the anger and disappoint she felt, hit her hard. That's when Diane had suggested she check into a wellness clinic in Denver that celebrities went to. Therapy had been a wake-up call, and Porscha fought her way back tooth and nail, although she hadn't done it by herself. She'd had help.

Xavier Lockett.

Sometimes just saying his name made her breath catch.

During her time at the clinic, they'd had a passionate affair, but Porscha had made the mistake of thinking it meant more. She'd thought they shared a connection. Then she'd overheard him discussing their relationship with another group member. He told the man that they were friends and nothing more. That was when she'd realized it had all been an illusion, but she'd been too caught up in the amazing sex to see the difference. Their breakup had been less than amicable.

It was why she limited her visits to Atlanta, because Xavier lived here. And for three years, she'd done good with only one visit to the stadium for a stop on her third album tour. But this? Singing the national anthem for the Atlanta Cougars was a recipe for disaster. There was a real possibility they could run into each other.

Although she'd done her best to steer clear of him, once in a while she looked Xavier up online to see what he was up to. He was a sports commentator for ASN and appeared to be doing well. She noticed that in the years since their breakup, he'd begun collecting women like trophies, showing them off at sports industry parties or high-profile events in Atlanta. Yet he never stayed with any of them for long. As soon as they lost their shiny newness, he discarded them, and it was on to the next best thing.

Porscha didn't have time for romance. Her career was her focus. She'd learned the hard way that she was a sucker when it came to men, so she'd been celibate. No man had ever aroused her passion like Xavier had.

She pushed Xavier out of her mind, determined to focus on the movie she was filming and its upcoming soundtrack. All she needed to do was change and get out of Lockett territory as fast as she could.

Xavier rushed past the locker rooms, physical therapy and recovery areas and arrived at the dressing rooms. Several bodyguards greeted him.

"Excuse me, sir. You're going to have to go back where you came from," one of the tall, beefy guards said, looking him up and down.

Luckily, Xavier still had his credentials on his lanyard and quickly showed them.

"I'm sorry, sir, I didn't realize you were one of the Locketts," the guard apologized. "Please…" He motioned Xavier forward.

"No worries. Where's Ms. Childs's room?" Xavier inquired. "I wanted to thank her for her rendition of the national anthem."

The guard led him down the hall to a door with a banner stating *Talent*.

"Thank you. I've got it from here." Xavier sucked in a breath and prepared himself for the less than enthusiastic greeting he was sure to receive. He and Porscha had broken up on bad terms. She thought he was a player using her for sex, but that had been far from true. They shared a bond and had gotten each other through the worst time in their lives.

Xavier knocked on the door. "Come in," a soft female voice said. He stepped inside the room and heard, "What the hell are *you* doing here?"

Porscha supposed she shouldn't be surprised. She'd known she could run into Xavier, but she didn't think he would seek her out because he hadn't in three years. And despite the surge of anger that sprang up from his sudden appearance, she had butterflies fluttering around in her tummy.

How was it possible he could *still* affect her like this?

In defiance of that revelation, she went with contempt. "I'll ask you again, what are you doing here?"

"I would think that's obvious," Xavier responded. "I came to see you."

"Ha!" Porscha laughed without humor.

Her mother rose from the couch she'd been sitting on. Diane Childs. She was tall with a slim build. She preferred trousers to dresses because they suited her more. She wore her hair in a sophisticated bob and preferred a swipe of lipstick and mascara to wearing any real makeup over her smooth fawn complexion. "Xavier Lockett, I presume?" she asked sizing him up.

"One and the same, ma'am."

"Then you know you shouldn't be here. Porscha is on a tight schedule."

"Perhaps, Porscha—" Xavier leaned sideways to glance behind Diane "—can speak for herself."

"I'm her manager."

"Mom, it's okay, I've got this." Porscha had a lot to say. Words she should have said three years ago.

Her mother turned to peer at her. "If you're sure?"

Porscha nodded. Diane stared at her for several seconds before she exited the room, leaving her and Xavier alone.

"It's good to see you. You look amazing," Xavier said.

"Of course, you'd say that." Porscha folded her arms across her bosom. "Because you were only interested in me for one thing."

"C'mon, Porscha. You know that's not true."

"Do I, Xavier?" she asked from a safe distance on the other side of the room because she knew she couldn't get any closer. Xavier had a way of pulling her in and she couldn't let that happen. She wasn't that easy. Or at least that was what she told herself.

"Yes, you do," he responded hotly. His eyes zeroed in on hers and Porscha found she couldn't look away. "It wasn't just physical. We helped get each other through a rough patch."

"That's not what you said back then."

"Because I wasn't about to put our business on blast to everyone in the clinic. It was private. Just between us."

"And you really expect me to believe that?" Porscha asked. "It's been three years, Xavier, and you've never tried to clear the air. So why now?"

"When I saw you upstairs on that television screen, I knew it wasn't over between us, Porscha." Xavier moved from the spot he'd been rooted to and strolled toward her. Porscha stepped backward until her hip hit the mirrored cabinet behind her. There was no place for her to run. "And seeing you up close and in person, I'm certain of it."

"You don't know what you're talking about."

"Maybe, but I don't think so," Xavier responded. "I haven't seen you date often over the last three years."

Porscha snorted. "Unlike you, who's been seen with lots of women."

Xavier smiled. "So you've been following me, huh?"

Porscha tossed her mane of jet-black curls over her shoulder. "Not really."

"Liar." He took a step toward her.

Porscha wanted to push him backward away from her, to batter his shoulders, but deep down she didn't want to.

So when he reached out and tunneled his hand through her hair, bringing her closer, she let him. He lowered his head and when she was inches away from his face, he said, "Tell me you don't want this." His tone was deep, smoky and sexy, causing a shiver to course down her spine.

Within seconds, she reached up and pulled him down toward her. Their mouths came together in an explosive kiss that sent a shock wave of lust through her body.

They kissed and kissed and kissed. Porscha tried to stay in the present, but the past merged with the present, flooding her with memories of how insatiable she'd once been for this man.

She refused to moan at the bliss of his kiss, but he tasted divine. When he used his tongue to lick across the seam of her lips, she opened to the demanding thrust of his tongue, relishing the erotic play. Xavier's lips were firm yet gentle, teasing hers until she gasped and whimpered, clinging to him. How was it that just one kiss from this man could make her frenzied with need? She could feel the place between her legs swell to life and moisten with excitement.

When Xavier pulled away, a craving for more built inside her. "Are we over, Porscha?" He looked down into her passion-glazed eyes and there was only one answer she could give.

No.

One

Six months later

"So nice of you to join us, Xavier," Vincent Chandler, the producer of Atlanta Sports Night, said when Xavier strolled into the rundown meeting on Monday, wearing a royal blue T-shirt and dark-washed jeans.

Xavier glanced down at his Rolex. "I'm sorry, am I late? The meeting is always at ten."

"I pushed it forward to nine thirty," Vincent responded. "And you'd know that if you looked at your texts."

Xavier rolled his eyes. He didn't need Vincent busting his chops. He'd come a long way the last few years from the rookie he'd been when he first joined the show.

It had taken him some time to find his footing. He was used to playing football, not commenting on it.

"Sorry," he shrugged and sat beside Marcus Elliot, his partner in crime on their show.

"Long night?" Marcus asked.

"You could say that," Xavier replied. He'd stayed up with a certain graceful R and B singer.

"In addition to your commentating," Vincent was saying, "we'd like you to do an in-depth interview with De'Sean Jones."

"Why me?" Xavier inquired. He wasn't the most seasoned sportscaster on the network. In fact, he was considered by most to be wet behind the ears. Why would they give him an interview with De'Sean, the biggest draft pick of the year, instead of Marcus?

"Because you know what it's like to be in his shoes," Vincent replied. "You won a Heisman."

Don't remind me, Xavier thought.

He'd tried his best to put those glory days behind him, but Vincent wasn't making this easy. "I really think Marcus would be better suited." Xavier understood interviews like this would advance his career, but he didn't want to be reminded of the life he'd once had but never would again. Plus, Xavier still struggled with whether sportscasting was the right place for him. Had he merely done his father's bidding?

"The network would like to switch things up a bit," Vincent explained. "They'd like to see a fresh perspective, and since you've lived a day in the life, we think you're the perfect candidate."

"I doubt that." Xavier laughed dryly.

"It wasn't a request," Vincent replied.

Xavier turned and glowered at him. Vincent had had it out for him since the moment he arrived at ASN. He'd heard rumors it had something to do with the fact Vincent had a commentator already picked but had been pushed to give Xavier the position because Xavier's father had an existing relationship with the head of ASN.

"Fine. Where and when?" Xavier asked.

Later, once Xavier made it back to his cubicle, Marcus stopped by. "Don't worry about anything, X. I've got you covered. I've done plenty of interviews."

"I know, but it should have been you," Xavier said, leaning back in his chair to regard him.

Marcus shrugged and leaned against the cubicle wall. "These things happen."

"It's not fair. You've done a lot to build this network." Xavier believed in paying your dues before you got your big break, like he'd done on the football field. But this world was much different than being on the field.

"That may be true. But if you want staying power in this business, you don't want to ruffle any feathers and you've got to know how to play the game. The network likes you. Leverage it to work in your favor."

After Marcus left, Xavier thought about his advice. Perhaps he was going about this all wrong. He'd always been bitter about his father helping him get the job. He didn't need anyone to fight his battles, but now that Xavier was in the driver's seat with the network, he could use them to raise his profile and garner support for his charity work. ASN had better get ready because things were about to change.

* * *

"Yes, like that, Porscha." The photographer gave her direction, and she dutifully angled her face into the flow of the air gushing from the wind machine, so her mane of sable hair wafted in a cloud around her. "Okay, give me sexy. A little more pout."

Porscha leaned in and tried to ignore her irritation and discomfort at how many times she had her makeup retouched and hair teased. She moved as she was told to move. She was a canvas for others to paint their vision of how they saw her. It was all part of the process. The photo shoot was for the soundtrack album cover for her new film with Ryan Mills. No doubt her face would be splashed across every magazine cover in the United States and beyond once the movie was released, because Ryan was extremely popular.

To get in the mood, Porscha daydreamed about Xavier and how he'd taken her up against the wall the night before. She'd been helpless to resist the raw, animal magnetism oozing from his every pore. She'd reveled in his powerfully naked body and the way he could extract every bit of pleasure from hers.

"Oh, yes, you've got it, Porscha. Just like that!"

After a half hour, the photo shoot ended and her personal assistant, Erin Connell, came by with a robe and wrapped it around Porscha's shoulders. "Thank you," Porscha said.

Erin was an affable young woman of average height, with fiery red hair and a sprinkling of freckles over her pale skin. She'd applied for the job as Porscha's assistant after graduating from UCLA with a degree in marketing. Her hope was to make it in the entertainment business someday, but initially she'd found it hard to get a job. Porscha had liked her immediately and hired her after the background check.

"You did great out there," her mother said from the sidelines.

"Thanks," Porscha replied as she walked toward the dressing room.

Ever since she and Xavier had picked up their affair again, she had been doing double duty flying between Atlanta and Los Angeles. She told her mother it was because of the soundtrack. That was partly true. At her request, the label had found a great producer in Atlanta to work on the soundtrack album, but that had ended a couple of months ago. She was doing the photo shoot here because of Xavier—because she couldn't get enough of him.

"What's next?" Porscha asked, glancing in her assistant's direction.

"You have an appearance at a radio station and that's it," Erin replied, leading Porscha to her dressing room.

Once there, Porscha stripped off her robe, even though her mother, Erin, Rachel Simone, her wardrobe stylist, and Kristen Love, her hair and makeup artist, were all in the room. She'd long ago given up any pretense of privacy in her world. These people were her glam squad, the team who ensured she always looked good. After her sophomore slump, Porscha refused to have any more unflattering photos of her published. It was why she never went in public without looking her best.

"Have you found a dress for the BET Awards?" Porscha asked, looking over at Rachel. She would be making an appearance on the awards show, the first of many appearances on the awards show circuit before the Grammys.

"No, but I will have a rack of options for you in a few days," Rachel replied. The blue-eyed blonde had a killer taste in fashion. Rachel usually dressed in designer clothes that would have seemed dowdy on Porscha, but on Rachel looked like she'd just come off the runway.

"Let's not leave it too late," Diane said, typing on her phone. "We want Porscha's ensemble to be talked about."

"Absolutely, Ms. Childs." Rachel knew her mother's lofty standards.

"But it's not the be-all and end-all," Porscha stated as Rachel helped her change into her street clothes.

Porscha was more concerned about her performance in her first film. She knew a lot of famous actresses had wanted the role, but in the end the director had chosen Porscha, an unproven talent, as the leading lady. As a result, she'd taken acting lessons because she was desperate to nail the story.

"Are you worried about the movie?" her mother inquired.

"Of course, Mama. It's my first. What if the critics think I'm terrible?"

Porscha had a love-hate relationship with the press. She considered the negativity part of the reason why she'd gone into a depression.

"I think you're doing fabulous."

Porscha laughed. "You have to say that. You're my mother."

"I agree with Diane," Erin interjected. "Your acting shows just the right amount of vulnerability."

"But we have to keep you in the spotlight," her mother continued. "This film could do for you what *The Bodyguard* did for Whitney Houston."

"Those are mighty big shoes to fill. I doubt anyone could," Porscha responded.

"Don't be defeatist. I didn't raise you to give up. You have to continue to elevate your game."

"How many more levels are there in this game?" Porscha sighed. "I'm exhausted. I feel like I'm in a never-ending game of Super Mario Brothers. When does it end?"

"When you stop being relevant," her mother replied. "When people stop buying your music. Baby girl, your third album, *Metamorphosis*, revitalized your career. And now you have the soundtrack. You must ride the wave. It's why Maybelline and L'Oréal came running and we have your new fragrance coming out next year. We need your brand diversified so if one part of your career slows, you have another to keep you afloat."

Porscha wondered if she meant keep *Diane Childs* afloat. Ever since her mother had discovered she could sing, it had been Porscha who kept the lights on and the rent paid once her father's financial support began to wane after he had other children. When she won prize money, it went to the coffers to take care of her, Diane said. But Porscha rarely saw any until she'd turned eighteen. That was when, with the help of the record label, she'd gotten an attorney and hashed out a manager contract with her mother.

Diane hadn't been happy about it, but Porscha was

tired of working her butt off and seeing very little reward. Now she knew where her money went without having to ask for a handout whenever she wanted to buy something.

"Can you have the car brought around?" Porscha asked Erin.

"Already done. I anticipated you wanted to get out of Dodge."

She most certainly did. She was in the mood to burn off some steam with her secret lover. She hoped he was up for it, because she had a lot of tension to get rid of.

"So how is the wedding planning coming?" Xavier asked Giana when he stopped by her and Wynn's home later that evening.

Eventually, his sister had gotten her man. She not only convinced Wynn Starks to sign a contract with the Cougars allowing the team to represent his sports drinks company, but while they were sparring over business, the two had fallen madly in love. After they'd gotten engaged on New Year's Eve, Giana had moved straight out of the Lockett family guesthouse and into Wynn's place. Luckily, he lived in Tuxedo Park, keeping Giana as the only girl child nearby their mother, who was practically giddy with excitement at finally having a wedding to plan. Both Xavier's brothers had put the cart before the horse. Their brides had been expecting when they put a ring on it and they'd both held small weddings.

"Xavier, Mama is driving me crazy," Giana said. "She wants it to be the wedding of the year." She used her hands to make air quotes. "You would think she would never get another opportunity. There's still you."

Xavier snorted. "Don't go talking blasphemy, Gigi. I'm content with my life."

Giana cocked her head to stare at him. "Are you really, Xavier? You've been seeing someone secretly for months. You don't want more?" His sister had discovered their affair when he'd come back to the family mansion late one night a few months ago.

"No," he lied. Although he wasn't looking for commitment, he wouldn't mind taking Porscha out on an official date—to a nice dinner or maybe even a movie—but she wasn't the average woman he dated. Porscha was a celebrity and with that came another set of rules. He understood why she wanted to keep their relationship a secret and avoid speculation. The last six months, he'd done things her way, and he'd enjoyed their trysts. The passion between them was off the charts.

"I don't believe you, Xavier," Giana said. "But I'm not going to push. I wasn't looking for love when Wynn came around. I just wanted the Atlanta Cougars to represent his sports drink LEAN."

"Well, you got your man," Xavier stated. "Just like you said you would."

A large grin spread across his sister's lips. "Yes, I did, and I couldn't be happier, but Wynn didn't make it easy."

"No, he didn't."

Xavier recalled how Wynn had flipped when he saw Giana meeting with his competitor Blaine Smith last December. He'd accused Giana of using their relationship as a way to get closer to him and instantly regretted his lack of trust in her. Eventually, he'd recruited Xavier's help to win his sister back.

It had worked.

"Are you happy, Xavier?" Giana inquired, regarding him. "And I don't mean with your secret lover because I can read between the lines."

Xavier shrugged. "What do you want me to say, Gigi? Nothing is ever going to replace football."

"Maybe instead of pushing it away, you should embrace it."

"C'mon, don't tell me you're on Dad's side and think I should coach the team?"

"That's not what I'm suggesting."

"Then what?" His family knew his feelings on the subject. He was never going to be the Xavier they remembered. Playing football had given him a purpose, and although he'd found an alternate life as a sportscaster, it wasn't the same. He'd *lived* to play the game.

"Don't get defensive, Xavier," Giana responded. "I was merely going to suggest you consider coming back to the Atlanta Cougars as a mentor to some of the younger players."

"A mentor?" The thought had never crossed his mind.

"Yes. You know what it's like to be in their shoes and the struggles they face in this business. You could give them advice on the pitfalls. And who knows, it could help you and them. What do you say?"

Xavier was about to say no, but Giana interrupted him. "And before you nix the idea, mull it over."

"I'll think about it."

"Why am I not convinced? I thought being at the clinic had brought you some peace."

"I wouldn't say that, but it helped me accept the things I couldn't change. Accept my limitations."

"You're only limited here—" Giana pointed to her temple "—if you let yourself be."

After he left Giana's, Xavier wondered if she was right, and he wasn't giving himself enough credit. Being a sports commentator left him a lot of free time, which he usually spent in the gym or helping the many charities at the Lockett Foundation.

He especially enjoyed the foundation's work with local and African orphanages to help ensure kids got the absolute best out of life, from the basics like food, clothing and shelter to an education. Xavier recognized how fortunate he was to come from privilege and never wanted to take it for granted. It was why he sat on the board of the foundation: he wanted to make a difference.

His mother had been proud when one of her children took up her charitable efforts, because his siblings had other focuses.

Roman and Giana were all about Atlanta Cougars business while Julian, as a sports doctor, took care of the players. But Xavier wanted to do more. During his brief time as the star quarterback, he'd donated half his earnings to charity. That hadn't changed once he became a sports commentator. His agent had helped secure a salary in the millions, which allowed him to continue his efforts.

Xavier was on his way home when his phone buzzed. Glancing down, he saw it was Porscha. "Hello?"

"Hi, it's me. Are you busy?" Porscha's silky voice asked from the other end of the line.

"No, I just left Giana's and was on my way home."

"I was hoping we could meet at our spot," she said. "It's been a tough day and I need a release."

Xavier laughed. "I can be there in twenty."

"Great, I'll see you soon." She was off the phone before he could say goodbye.

Twenty minutes later, he was pulling his Porsche convertible up to the gate. He'd recruited his good friend John Summers, who'd sold Roman his house last year, to find them a secret hideaway. And John had come through. The location was in an upper-class neighborhood with complete privacy and security. Xavier walked up the paved driveway and punched in the code and the door opened.

Flicking on the light, he quickly used the alarm code she'd given him to turn off the security system. He glanced around the house, which was tastefully decorated in beige and earth tones. He walked inside and made himself comfortable in the nicely appointed kitchen, complete with a small bar in a nook near the living room. He found his favorite Scotch and prepared a drink while he waited for Porscha.

In most of his relationships, Xavier set the pace. This time, however, Porscha wanted to be in charge, and he'd accepted it because she awakened a ferocious lust he hadn't felt with other women.

He didn't have to wait long for her arrival. Within a half hour, he saw lights in the driveway, and seconds later, Porscha walked through the front door.

"Can you wait out here, Jose?"

"Absolutely, ma'am," he heard a male voice say.

Porscha came toward him dressed in a sexy gold mesh top that showed off her round breasts, a fringed miniskirt that barely covered her bottom, and some high-heeled booties showing off her shapely legs. She looked hot.

"Wow!" Xavier couldn't stop ogling.

She grinned, spinning around. "I'm glad you approve, but this getup was entirely for my mother's benefit, to make her believe I was going out with friends instead of my real agenda, which was coming here."

"I take it she wouldn't approve?"

"I don't care if she approves or not. I'm here because I want to be." She reached behind her, and to his surprise the mesh top she'd been wearing fell to the floor, revealing her bare bosom underneath.

Xavier swore.

He closed the gap between them with slow but sure steps, fixing her with a heated stare. Her nipples beaded as he approached. He cupped the small weight of her swelling breasts, thumbed the cresting peaks, and then lowered his head to feast on one stiff nipple. Porscha threw her head back and let him take his fill. He tugged and suckled her steadily until her back arched.

He finally lifted his head and said, "Do you know how beautiful you are?"

She smiled at his praise. "You don't have to say that."

His finger traced her lower lip. "Don't doubt it. Because you are." Her eyelids lowered. Xavier remembered Porscha's insecurities about her body, but she was perfect in every way to him, and he would remind her tonight and any other night she let him.

He dropped to his knees and pulled down the mini-skirt and the scarlet thong in one fell swoop. He looked up at her as he cupped her bare bottom. "Missed me?"

"Yes," she croaked. Her eyes were glazed with passion because she matched his ardor.

"Let's see how much," Xavier replied and put one of her legs over his shoulders. "I can't wait to taste you." Then he lowered his head so he could reacquaint himself with the place between her thighs.

"Ohmigod!" Porscha let out a loud sigh and clung to Xavier's shoulders for support. Her daydreams about how good the sex with Xavier was didn't do the man justice. There was no thought of shyness or self-consciousness. Instead, she abandoned herself completely to every stroke of Xavier's tongue and fingers inside her wet heat. Teasing, licking, flicking and swirling, Xavier brought her to the edge using all the skills she'd never been able to forget.

He made her cross boundaries she never would have before—like coming to this house so scantily clad. If she had her way, she'd dress in sweats, but the music business required she show off more skin than she was comfortable with. But Xavier always exulted in her body and made her want to show off the progress she'd made. Since leaving Colorado, she'd gotten to her target weight that was managed by a personal chef who ensured she ate a balanced diet and a trainer who had her on a rigorous exercise regime.

And now she could feel comfortable with the man who gave her powerful orgasms.

"Xavier!" She cried his name when her climax

struck, trembling and quaking as she came face-to-face
with the oblivion she craved. Gazing down at him, she
saw a smoky, sensual pride gleaming in his brown eyes.

"Are you ready for round two?" Xavier inquired.

Before she could answer, he rose and swept her le-
thargic body into his arms and headed to the bedroom.

He strode down the hall with her in his arms as if
she weighed nothing. Then he was pressing her down
onto the coverlet of the master bed, drawing it back so
he could lay her on the cool sheets. Porscha watched
with amazement as Xavier stripped off his clothes and
sheathed himself. His desire for her was blatant and she
welcomed it; she couldn't wait to run her palms across
his smooth and muscled torso. And when he joined her
on the bed, she did exactly that.

When he flattened her breasts against his hard chest,
she ran her hands over his back, glorying in its muscled strength. She loved his full build, broad shoulders
and ample behind. She reached behind him to grip his
butt, bringing them skin to skin. "I need you inside
me, *now*," she moaned and opened her thighs wider.
"Please, give me what I want."

"I'm happy to oblige." He leaned over her and
pushed his body into hers in one sure, swift stroke.
Porscha undulated beneath him, and Xavier's hips
rocked as he settled into a fast, hard rhythm that she
eagerly matched.

He pressed a kiss to the side of her neck and began
taking nips of her earlobe. Porscha shuddered as passion and pleasure rushed through her. "Oh, yes, like
that!"

* * *

Xavier fought to regain control as Porscha took him deeper inside her. He was large, but her muscles clamped around him, milking him and drawing him in fully.

His release was so close, but it was too soon. He wanted to draw out the moment, but his skin was rippling with goose bumps. He slipped his hand down between them to delve inside her wet heat and Porscha gave a high-pitched cry of pleasure. Xavier closed his eyes as shock waves coursed through her and detonated inside of him, sucking his last vestige of control. He gripped her tightly and began pumping hard.

Porscha's body welcomed his and when she squeezed his butt and locked her legs around his hips, it was over. He took her mouth in a hard, deep kiss, swallowing her cries as another round of tremors erupted through her. Only then did he surrender and tumble over the edge of the world, with Porscha around him cushioning him as he fell.

They stayed together like that in each other's arms until eventually she drifted off to sleep. That was when Xavier rose from the bed and headed to the shower. He and Porscha never spent the night together.

Her rules.

Not his.

They'd fallen fast and quick their first time around and neither of them was eager for a repeat performance. Porscha didn't trust him, had believed the worst of him, and that hurt more than he'd ever let on. Xavier was willing to continue their physical relationship because they were compatible in bed, but he refused to go deeper for fear that if he wasn't careful, he would fall headlong into disaster again with this woman, and his heart couldn't take another beating. He kept Porscha at arm's length just like she wanted, and in so doing, he protected his heart.

Two

"Good morning, Ma," Xavier said when he came to the breakfast table the next morning, wearing a T-shirt and sweatpants. She was in the morning room alone drinking a cup of coffee while perusing the news on her tablet.

He lived at home with his parents in the separate wing of the house. When he'd been the Cougars quarterback and always on the road, Xavier hadn't seen the need for his own place. And after the injury, he'd been depressed, and having family nearby helped. He didn't have to cook or clean for himself and generally his parents left him to his own devices. Plus with his siblings hitched, his mother loved having one of her children nearby so she could be a mother hen.

"Good morning. Did you sleep well?" Angelique

Lockett was an ageless beauty with a peanut butter complexion and light brown eyes. She looked flawless in slender slacks and a flowery tunic. Her normally shoulder-length jet-black hair was in a carefully blown, sleek chignon.

"Yes, I did." Xavier had been exhausted by last night's extracurricular activities. When he finally came home, he'd passed out.

"What do you have planned for today?" his mother asked. Since it was off-season now for football, his agent wanted him to meet with several networks about coming on board as a game analyst for other sports. And Xavier intended to, but he was more interested in his charitable projects.

"I hope it's coming to the stadium to talk to the head coach, John Russell," his father said, walking into the room before Xavier could get a word in edgewise. "It's not too late to get you in for next season."

"C'mon, Dad. I told you I don't want a coaching position."

"It's only because you're afraid to get back in the saddle. You need to get over your fear."

"Stop it!" Xavier shouted, slamming his palm against the table and causing the dishes on top to rattle. "Can't I enjoy my breakfast in peace? If that's not possible, I'll happily move out. I've stayed here much too long anyway. With Giana gone, it's not the same." He hadn't felt the need to leave before, but the longer he and Porscha continued their fling, the more he realized he needed his own space.

"Darling, no!" His mother leaned over and touched

his hand. "Please don't go." She scowled at his father. "We don't want you to. Do we, Josiah?"

His father rolled his eyes and reached for the coffee carafe to pour himself a cup of joe. "The boy is a grown man, Angie. If he wants to move out, let him. He's not your baby boy anymore."

"He'll always be my baby." His mother smiled in Xavier's direction. "Even when you're old and gray."

Xavier appreciated his mother trying to lighten the mood, but it was time for him to move on. "How about this? I'll move into the guesthouse. In the meantime, I'm heading to the Lockett Foundation. I'm meeting with the director of the youth complex we're building for after-school athletic programs and summer camps."

The foundation helped support several youth organizations within the Atlanta community by providing new uniforms and athletic equipment to underprivileged kids, but the complex they'd just built was a huge win for the community.

"I'm so proud of you, Xavier. You're the only one of my children who's taken up the baton with the foundation," his mother replied.

"Thanks, Ma." Xavier kissed her cheek and made a swift exit. He needed to leave before his father continued to press him about coming on as an assistant coach with the Atlanta Cougars. Once again, Josiah was trying to tell him what to do. He probably felt entitled because all his life Xavier had followed the path his father laid out. Football. Football. And more football.

Those days, however, were over. Xavier was his own man now, with his own thoughts and ideas about the direction of his life. And when he was ready to make his next move, he would. But it wouldn't be because the great Josiah Lockett ordained it.

"Right this way," the announcer said as Porscha, her mom, Erin and the rest of her team walked down the hall toward the stage for the Lois Howard talk show several days later in New York.

In between filming her new movie, Porscha had several appearances lined up to sing a popular hit off her third album. She was sitting down with Lois on her popular syndicated talk show for a Q and A. Since Lois was known for asking guests to dance, Porscha had made sure her ensemble—of an oversize, abstract-print blazer with a deep V cut and skinny capris with high-heeled booties—was not only chic and flattering to her figure, but nimble enough for her to do a few dance moves.

Once they arrived backstage, Kristen powdered her nose to take off any shine, but it was her mother who fiddled with her outfit, brushing off invisible lint and making sure not a hair was out of place. When her name was announced and the soft strands of one of her most popular ballads, "The One Who Loves You," came on, Porscha sashayed onstage.

Bright lights and a lone spotlight greeted Porscha along with an in-person studio audience, but she blocked it out of her mind. Instead, she focused on the beautiful lyrics, letting the music take her along the journey. The song started off slow and quiet, allowing her to look at the audience and connect with them. But as the melody grew stronger and the song came to its crescendo, so did Porscha's voice. She opened her arms, sweeping them wide as the note climbed with the music.

Her eyes closed as she sang the last refrains of the song. When she opened them and looked out over the audience, she saw tears in the eyes of several people right before she bowed.

Applause erupted.

The cameras cut to a commercial break.

Lois, holding several index cards in her hand, came out to greet Porscha. "That was amazing!" Her platinum blonde hair was neatly pulled back into a ponytail, and she wore a simple white silk blouse, black slacks and low heels.

Porscha beamed with pride. "Thank you."

"No, seriously, your voice is like warm syrup over pancakes," Lois responded.

Porscha laughed. "I don't think I've ever been described that way. Do you mind if I powder my nose?"

"No, of course not. We'll be back in five minutes."

Porscha rushed off the stage and found her mother and Kristen waiting to touch up her makeup and fix her hair.

"That was great, Porscha, really," her mother said. "Though next time, I would like to see you hold that last note just a bit longer, you know, milk the crowd for all their worth."

Porscha narrowed her eyes. Her mother wasn't a singer, but she certainly could be critical of a skill she'd never acquired. "Thanks, I'll remember that."

After a quick brush of powder, she was back on set with the talk show host. Lois was funny and charming, and Porscha could see why her show was popular around the globe. "How's the filming of your new movie with Ryan Mills going?" Lois inquired.

"It's fantastic," Porscha gushed. "To work with someone of his caliber is wonderful, especially for my first film."

"Were you nervous when you first met him?"

Porscha knew exactly what to do. She had to stroke her costar's ego. He'd been voted Sexiest Man Alive by People *twice* in the last decade. "Oh, absolutely! I'm his biggest fan!"

When the time came, Lois didn't hesitate to ask Porscha to show one of her best dance moves and she was ready. Porscha knew her limitations. She was no dancer, but she executed a few shakes and wiggles of her hips that she'd practiced with her choreographer. It appeased Lois and before she knew it, the interview was over.

"Everyone, let's give Porscha Childs a big thank-you for coming on the show," Lois said, clapping her hands.

The audience not only gave her a roaring applause, but a standing ovation as well. Porscha was humbled. It felt great to be on top again. She'd taken it for granted with her first album, thinking the public's goodwill would last forever. It had been humiliating when her sophomore album bombed. The press hadn't been kind. In fact, they'd been downright brutal about the weight she had gained with her depression and grief over losing her father.

Once offstage, Porscha didn't go back to the green room but followed her mother and Erin toward the rear exit, where a car was waiting outside. She saw a crowd of fans had gathered to see her. Many of them were holding up posters with her picture and the magazine she'd recently been featured on.

"Porscha, you don't have time for this," her mother whispered in her ear.

"Yes, I do," Porscha hissed, pulling away. "They're my fans." With a smile on her face, she walked over to the group, and her bodyguard Jose joined her.

"Ohmigod, I love you, Porscha!" a young man gushed when she approached. "Can I have a picture?"

"Sure." Porscha leaned in for a quick selfie. Then she autographed several more photos and a magazine before waving and heading back to the car.

Jose held open the door and Porscha slid inside. Her mother was waiting for her but didn't harangue. She pivoted to a new topic. "Great interview, Porscha. The media ate up how you gushed over Ryan."

Porscha frowned. "I didn't gush."

Her mother shrugged as she looked down at her phone. "Doesn't matter. An audience member already tweeted about it and there's speculation that the two of you are an item."

"They got all of that from me saying I'm a huge fan of Ryan's?" Porscha rolled her eyes upward. "That's crazy."

They arrived at the popular NYC hotel where they were staying, and once again, she was greeted by a flock of paparazzi and fans. Reaching inside her bag for her compact, Porscha checked her face and hair one more time before exiting the vehicle.

She smiled in front of the cameras, but Porscha wondered if anyone ever really saw her. The *real* her. Certainly not her mother, who was only interested in the image Porscha presented to the world and how it affected their pocketbook. Once her mother realized she had talent at an early age, she'd pushed Porscha to ensure her daughter would live up to *her* wildest dreams. The only one who had ever seemed to really want to get to know Porscha was Xavier.

Porscha walked into the hotel in a daze and thought back to when they had been at the clinic. She'd let Xavier in, allowed him to see the real her without all the trappings. And she didn't mean just hair or makeup, though back then she had taken out her weave and worn her hair in its natural state. But more than that, she'd shared her fears and dreams and he'd listened. For the first time in a long time, she thought someone cared about her.

That was why it hurt when he'd indicated that they were friends and nothing more. He devalued their relationship and it had wounded not only her heart, but her pride. She'd vowed never to give a man that kind of power over her again, especially after what happened with her ex-boyfriend Gil Harris. Six years ago, she'd foolishly believed Gil cared for her, too, but he'd only been using her for fame and fortune. As soon as a big payday came, he'd dropped Porscha like a hot potato. She'd been heartbroken and looked like a fool to the world after talking about how madly in love with him she was.

Xavier's reemergence in her life threw her. She'd wanted to act as if she didn't care, but the passion she felt for him was still there. And when he kissed her, she'd been as lost as she had been three years ago. She'd fallen in love with him then, but her feelings were not returned. This time, she'd told herself that if they had a fling, she could rid herself of the long-buried feelings she had for him.

That had been six months ago.

She was no closer to figuring out where her emotions stood. Instead, whenever she felt herself spinning out of control and needing an anchor, she called Xavier. She could talk to him about anything, and he listened. *Had she gotten it wrong all those years ago?*

No, no, this was a fool's mission. She was going down the same road and expecting a different result. Sure, he talked to her on the phone, but in all the times they'd been intimate, not once had Xavier mentioned wanting more than sex. He played up his single lifestyle in his social media. What was she supposed to think? She had to stop yearning for something she would never have and focus on her career, because it was all she had.

"You really have a knack for this, Xavier," Andrew Chapman, director of the Lockett Foundation, stated once the room cleared out of their weekly meeting that afternoon.

"I'm really passionate about what we do here."

Ever since Xavier was a high school senior and had gone to an away game and seen the conditions other teams played in, he'd wanted to make a difference. Once he'd been drafted, Xavier realized his platform could help further causes he was interested in. He used part of his earnings to support those charities. And after he discussed it with his mother, she'd agreed the foundation would help with his efforts.

"We are certainly lucky to have you," Andrew said.

"I have to head into another meeting, but I'll talk to you later."

Xavier nodded. He was on his way to his office when he decided to make a U-turn and head to the medical clinic on the lower level of the foundation's offices. Usually, Julian volunteered there during the off-season.

Opening the clinic door, he found his brother in the reception area, chatting with one of the staff members. "Xavier!" Julian smiled when he entered and came from around the counter to greet him. "What brings you to this neck of the woods?"

"Can't I come see my brother?"

"Of course, but you don't usually come down to interact with the lower rung of the family."

Xavier laughed, ignoring Julian's dig, and gave him a hug. "How's it going?"

"I saw a few patients earlier, but it's been a slow day."

"Care to take a walk?"

"Of course." Julian turned and glanced back at the receptionist. "Call me if you need me."

"Sure thing, boss," she replied, giving him a salute.

Julian followed Xavier down the hall. They were both silent until they were out of earshot of others and outside walking the grounds.

"What's on your mind?" Julian asked.

"Dad. He keeps pushing me to join the coaching staff."

"I thought that was a moot point. You said no."

"I did. I refuse to let Dad run roughshod over me. He's always pushed me, you know?"

"He did that to all of us, Xavier," Julian responded,

sitting on a nearby bench. "When he wasn't putting a football in your hand, he was placing Roman as an intern with the Cougars and making sure he learned the business from the ground up. After Rome, I was next, but I didn't fit the mold of the son he envisioned. I was always more Mama's child, into arts and culture."

"How did you handle that?" Xavier joined him on the bench.

"I rebelled. I did things just to spite Josiah. But did that stop him? No, if I wasn't going to play ball, I was going into sports medicine. He was determined I have a role with the organization. And surprisingly, I found I enjoyed it. I could help the players and still not feel like an outsider in my own family."

"You felt like an outcast?"

Julian laughed. "Now, there's the understatement of the year, but this isn't about me. I made my peace with Josiah, and we live in a comfortable truce. Now that I have Elyse, I don't sweat the small stuff anymore. But you, you've always been the apple of his eye."

"That's the problem, Julian. It's hard to live up to this idealized version Dad has in his mind of me. I'm never going to be a quarterback again."

"True, but you are gifted, Xavier. You always have been. Whenever they put that football in your hand, you knew exactly what to do with it. You shouldn't sell yourself short."

"I don't do that."

"Yes, you do. Look at what you've done with the Lockett Foundation."

"I couldn't mope forever," Xavier responded. Giving back to those less fortunate helped put his position in perspective. He was young, in relatively good health, and had a lifetime ahead of him. So what if he walked with a slight limp? "I've learned not to let football define me, and I'm afraid if I go back, it will suck me into this vortex of negativity because I can't get out there and play myself."

Julian nodded. "I can see where that would give you pause. But sometimes helping others is its own reward."

"Agreed. I've decided to step my foot back into the organization and take Giana up on her offer to mentor some of the younger players."

"That's fantastic! I'm sure she'll be pleased."

"I'm not doing it for her."

Xavier was doing it for himself, because he suspected it would help him move forward to recapturing the man he used to be.

"How did it go today?" Xavier asked Porscha later that night as she lay in her New York hotel room. Somehow this had become their routine when they were apart, or she was on the road. They would call each other and talk for hours about everything and nothing. Sometimes the calls were naughty, which was why Porscha was in a baby doll nightie right now.

"The song went fantastic, and Lois was wonderful. She made me feel at ease, so I was able to talk about my music."

"I know how much that means to you."

"Sometimes I think my mom forgets that at the end of the day all I have ever wanted to do is sing. All she talks about is my brand and expanding my reach. I mean this acting thing, it wasn't my idea, you know?"

"Then why don't you speak up? Tell her how you feel?"

Because Porscha was afraid. She knew how much her success meant to her mother. She'd sacrificed a lot to ensure Porscha had everything she needed to achieve her dream. But how long did Porscha have to pay the debt?

"I don't know," Porscha said. "She's done so much for me."

"Yeah, but you don't owe her your entire life. It's up to you to choose what's best for you."

"I don't see you putting your foot down and telling Josiah in no uncertain terms that you don't want to coach," Porscha countered defensively.

"Are you trying to start a fight, Porscha?" His curt voice lashed at her. "Because this wasn't about me."

"No, I'm not spoiling for an argument," she sighed. "But I'm also pointing out what we share in common. Two domineering parents who think they know what's best for us."

"*We* have to put them in their place."

"And how's that working for you?" Porscha inquired.

"No better than you," Xavier admitted honestly, and she appreciated he wasn't afraid of speaking his truth. "But at least I have my work at the foundation. I love what I do there. If I were to go to back to football, it would take away from my charity work."

"*You* have to decide what's more important to you, Xavier. Don't try to fit yourself into the image others have of you and deny who or what you've become. Our therapy taught us to face our fears and that's what you have to do."

They ended the call soon after, with Xavier still being miffed by her words, but Porscha refused to take them back. She knew it was unfair. She talked a good game, but could she heed her own advice? Could she stand up to her mother and tell her what *she* wanted and how *she* wanted to run her career? The task seemed daunting, so the little girl within pulled the covers over her head and fell asleep.

Three

"I have to say I'm not surprised," Giana said when Xavier strolled into the Atlanta Cougars managers meeting in the corporate headquarters conference room on Monday morning in a shirt and tie. He was fifteen minutes early.

He needed the extra time to deal with coming to the corporate headquarters. Xavier hadn't been back here since the injury that ended his career, but he had to face his own demons. And when he'd walked the halls just now, it felt like coming home, but it was also bittersweet because he was a visitor instead of a player.

This place had felt more like home than the family mansion in Tuxedo Park. He'd grown up here. From practicing as a teen in the youth camps to eventually running plays as a quarterback, it was part of his DNA.

But he'd turned his back on it the last few years. He had to for his own self-preservation—until he could come to terms with the fact he'd never play ball again.

"Don't be smug," Xavier finally said, sitting by her side at the table.

"Why not?" Giana quirked a brow and glanced sideways at him. "I can't bask in the win? I told you mentoring was a promising idea and now everyone else will know it, too."

"Know what?" Roman asked, coming into the room. "What'd I miss?" He looked every bit the role of general manager in a bespoke navy suit with a blue-and-silver-striped tie. His smooth chocolate skin was similar to Giana's, but he had an expertly shorn beard.

"That Xavier is coming back to the team," Giana replied.

"In a limited capacity," Xavier added. He didn't want his family to put the cart before the horse. He'd thought long and hard about the advice Julian and Porscha gave him. And at the end of the day, he realized that helping others was something he did well. If he could offer new Cougars players some sound wisdom, he would.

"Nonetheless, we're happy to see you here, little brother," Roman said with a grin.

And looking into his brother's ebony eyes, Xavier believed him. Rome had been raised to be heir apparent and the role suited him, but he'd never hung it over any of their heads or made his siblings feel less than. He always played fair, which made him a great leader.

The rest of the department heads eventually trickled in, but their father wasn't one of them. Xavier was surprised the old man was actually letting go of the reins as he'd promised. It had been a source of friction between him and Roman last year, but their father had stepped down as general manager. Now Roman was running the show and Giana was his number two.

His brother got the meeting underway, and he and Giana spoke about what was coming next in the off-season. They'd had a successful scouting combine a few weeks ago and had their eyes on a few players who performed at top physical and mental condition. There was a lot of talk of the draft this month and what it would take to secure the players they needed.

Xavier was amazed. He'd never been privy to the behind-the-scenes of how football teams recruited players because he'd been on the field. There was a lot of wheeling and dealing, and Roman and Giana were more than up to the task. Eventually the meeting agenda ventured to new business. Giana brought up the mentorship program. When she made the announcement that Xavier would lead the effort, there were loud whispers among the department heads. Xavier had steered clear of any role in the Cougars since he'd retired from being a quarterback. Eventually, it was the head coach, John Russell, who spoke up.

"Do you really think that's a good idea?" John asked.

"I think it's a mighty fine proposal, John," Roman said, and he would have gone further, but Xavier stood and faced all the naysayers in the room. Some of them knew how tough it had been for Xavier to walk away from the game. There had been rumors he'd gone to a rehab facility that specialized in more than just ensuring he could walk again. They probably wondered if he was the right person to mentor other players.

"All of you know me," Xavier started, glancing around the table. "You watched me grow up on the field. You saw my successes and my failures. And yes, when I failed, it was spectacular. But that's also why I'm uniquely qualified to talk to new players about the pitfalls of success and how to keep themselves healthy. If you're looking for a poster child of the perfect football player, you won't find it in me." He looked around the room. "But I can tell them how to get back up when they fall."

John stared at him for a long time. Xavier knew he understood because John had played football, too, and Xavier had been a huge fan. He'd watched John's reels on many occasions, hoping that one day he could live up to his legacy. And for a brief time, he had.

"Then I'm on board," John replied. "Welcome back, Xavier."

John had no idea how much his words of encouragement meant to Xavier. And he told him so later after the meeting wrapped.

"I think it's great," John added. "You have a lot of advice you can offer some of these players. But I'm curious what made you decide to come back now."

Xavier thought about a petite singer on the other side of the country. She'd given him the final push he needed when she'd asked how long he was going to continue to deny his passion.

"I got a little push."

Later that morning, Porscha sat obediently in her trailer on the film set and watched as her mother took the hash browns off her breakfast plate of egg whites, grilled tomato and grapefruit. She rolled her eyes. She hated when Diane clocked what she ate, but Porscha knew she had to stay off carbs. They were not her friend and went straight to her hips.

"'Forever Love' is getting great coverage," her mother said. "It's in heavy rotation on all the major radio stations. It's going to be as big a hit as 'My Heart Will Go On' was for Celine Dion."

Porscha grinned. "That's wonderful news."

"We have to continue to capitalize on the moment," her mother stated. "Between the soundtrack and this film, who knows? You could be up for an Oscar and a Grammy next year."

"You really think so?"

"Absolutely."

As a young girl, she'd wanted to win a Grammy, and later she had, with her first album, more than one, but her second album hadn't produced a Billboard hit. Luckily, she'd rebounded, and the record label's hope that lightning would strike twice had been fulfilled. Her third album was a critical success and garnered several top singles along with another two Grammys. Her single "Forever Love" for the film's soundtrack was poised to do even better. Porscha knew it the moment she'd heard the song, but an Oscar? She hadn't wanted to dream too big, but perhaps it was possible to have it all?

A knock sounded on her trailer door and the production assistant poked his head in. "Porscha, we're ready for you."

"Be right there." She smoothed down the dress she'd be wearing in the scene.

"Knock their socks off, Porscha," Erin said. Her assistant was always there to give Porscha a boost when she needed it.

"Thanks, Erin."

Her mother stayed behind because Porscha told her having her on set made Porscha nervous and she didn't want to flub her lines. Diane hadn't liked it—she always wanted to be in the thick of the action where her daughter was concerned, but Porscha had been adamant.

When she left the trailer, Porscha followed the production assistant over to the set. Ryan was already there and smiled as she approached. With his light brown skin, curly hair and neat goatee, Ryan was easy on the eyes. Porscha could see why he was considered a heartthrob. Although slightly under six feet, he boasted an athletic build.

"You ready for this?" Ryan asked, ignoring the person dabbing makeup on his face.

"Yes." Porscha put on a good front to belie the inner turmoil roiling her tummy. Although they'd been on set for several weeks, Porscha still got nervous when it was time to film. It might come easy for Ryan but acting was new to her.

"I want to thank you for the positive press," Ryan said with a grin. "I never knew you had such a crush on me."

Porscha laughed at his cockiness. "Don't go getting a big head. That was purely for show."

"Ouch. You mean to tell me you don't want to marry me and have my babies like the tabloids say?" he teased.

Porscha shook her head. "Afraid not."

He clutched his heart. "You've wounded me."

"Positions, everyone!" the director yelled.

Ryan rose from his chair and they both got on their markers, and soon the cameras were rolling. Porscha forgot about where she was and transported herself into the role of an aspiring singer who meets Ryan, a talent manager at a local nightclub. They fall in love as he helps her with her career, but he's killed tragically in a robbery. Her character finds a way to go on without him and make a success of herself because that was what he would have wanted.

"Cut!" the director yelled. "That was wonderful, Porscha. Really fantastic job. We'll take a fifteen-minute break and come back."

Porscha exited the soundstage and walked to Erin, who waited with her phone. "Thanks." She took the device and noticed she'd missed a text from Xavier.

Break a leg.

Xavier knew how hard acting was for her. Porscha searched for an empty room and stepped inside, closing the door. She leaned against it and took a deep, cleansing breath. She'd done it. It wasn't easy pretending that she knew what she was doing. She dialed Xavier.

"How was the scene?" he asked without preamble.

"Good. I was nervous, but it's getting easier."

"Told ya. You have nothing to worry about. You're a natural."

"You're biased," she responded. One evening, when she'd been in Atlanta, she'd been nervous about an up-coming scene and Xavier had offered to run lines with her. He'd been complimentary, but Porscha wasn't sure she could believe him. He was sleeping with her after all.

"Yeah, well, I know talent when I see it," Xavier shot back hotly.

"And you? Did you decide about the mentorship?" She was curious if Xavier had gone along with his sister's suggestion that he mentor the younger members of the Atlanta Cougars.

"I did."

"And? Don't make keep me in suspense."

"I said yes." She heard the smile in Xavier's voice, and it made her happy. She wanted that for him— wanted him to do what he was passionate about.

"I'm glad."

"Then perhaps you'll agree to help with a special project of mine?" Xavier asked. "I wasn't going to ask, but I need a favor. We had a local artist drop out of singing at the opening of the Lockett Foundation's new youth center and I need a replacement."

Porscha frowned. Why hadn't he asked *her* to perform first? She would have attended if her schedule permitted. That was what she didn't understand. Sometimes they acted like a couple, calling and texting each other, but other times, Xavier acted as if she didn't exist, like going elsewhere for talent when he could come to her.

"If it's too much trouble, I can ask someone else," Xavier said when she remained silent on the other end of the line.

"I can do it."

"You're upset with me?" Xavier asked, intuitively

understanding her reluctance. "Because I didn't ask you first. I'm sorry, Porsch. I didn't want you to think you owed me anything because…because we're sleeping together."

"I would never think that. So next time, ask me. What's the date?"

"Friday. Are you free?"

"I have to be back on set Monday, but I'll make it work."

"Thanks, Porscha. The kids are going to be so excited."

"You know I would do anything for children," Porscha responded and ended the call. What she really wanted to say was that she'd do anything for Xavier, but they weren't in a place where they could say that to each other.

Never had been.

She'd defined the parameters of their affair and she had to stick to the terms. Otherwise it would only confuse them both.

There was a knock. "Porscha, they are ready for you back on set," the production assistant said from the other side of the door.

Porscha opened the door. "Let's do it."

Xavier put the phone down on his desk. He got the distinct impression Porscha was miffed because he hadn't asked her first, to do the appearance. They didn't have that kind of relationship. He'd agreed to be Porscha's plaything on the side and because he wanted her, he'd accepted the terms.

He'd thought the chemistry between them would

burn itself out like most of his relationships. Before Porscha, Xavier kept women at a distance because nothing could come between him and football, his first real love. So his dealings with the opposite sex were of the physical variety, and after a release, it was on to the next one. But then he met Porscha, and he lost his head. He could remember the first time they'd been together.

After taking a long walk together at the facility in Colorado, he'd taken a blanket from his room and spread it on the grass in a secluded spot. Then they'd undressed and he'd found everything he didn't know he'd been looking for. It made Xavier wonder if they could give this long-distance relationship a try even though he lived in Atlanta and she lived in Los Angeles.

However, when she overheard him at the clinic talking to another group member, she'd gotten it all wrong. He hadn't been about to share his confidence with the man or confirm or deny his assumptions. At the time, Porscha had been under a heavy amount of scrutiny. He would never kiss and tell, so he said they were friends and there was nothing between them.

Then he'd turned around and seen Porscha standing in his doorway. The hurt expression in her eyes told him she'd heard every word. Xavier tried to apologize, but all she could hear was that she didn't mean anything to him. She accused him of using her to get through his time at the clinic. Her words had been like acid because they hadn't been true. He'd retaliated by stating she used him for the orgasms he gave her. The moment he said the words Xavier had regretted them because Porscha stepped backward as if he'd struck her.

It was a low blow and not in his nature, but once they were out there, he couldn't take them back.

Porscha told him they were over. She never wanted to see him and then she'd walked out of his life. Porscha Childs was one of Xavier's biggest regrets. *She* was the one who got away. Was that why, since his stint in the clinic, he'd become even more guarded? Every time a woman tried to get close, his walls came up. The closest Xavier had ever gotten to feeling he could love someone was with Porscha.

Which was why there was going to come a point when the two of them would have *the talk* and find out where they wanted this affair to go. But for now he would leave things as they were.

Four

"Porscha, the press is eating up this bit about you and Ryan," her mother said. "It hasn't died down. We really should be playing this up."

"But it's not true," Porscha returned. "We're not dating."

"Does it matter? Why are you fighting me on this?" her mother asked in the limo on the way to Xavier's grand opening event for his youth complex on Friday afternoon. "It would be great press for you."

The media were claiming she and Ryan were an item. For the last half hour since they landed at the airport, her mother had been suggesting Porscha go along with the story to boost her career. After her interview with Lois, the rumor had gained traction and was picked up by several national entertainment outlets.

"Is it because of your relationship with Xavier?"

Porscha had had to confide in her mother about her relationship with Xavier because she'd been relentless in wanting to know why they kept coming back to Atlanta and why Porscha was singing at some "random" youth complex. She wished she hadn't told her mother, because she harped on the fact Xavier wasn't as famous as Ryan.

She'd defended Xavier when her mother called him washed-up. Porscha explained his family were Atlanta royalty and owned the Atlanta Cougars, but Diane countered that he was a small fish. They'd gone round and round until her mother realized Porscha wasn't changing her mind and she'd better get used to Xavier being a fixture in her life.

But today, Diane Childs was in rare form. She wanted Porscha to go out on a date with Ryan to fuel the gossip flames and hopefully boost sales of the soundtrack single. It wasn't a bad idea, but Porscha didn't like her mother thinking she had the final say.

"This has nothing to do with my relationship with Xavier," Porscha said, returning to her earlier comment. "We're not together like that." She was still hurt that he'd only asked her to sing at the event because another artist had dropped out. That stung. She thought they were friends as well as lovers.

"What are you saying?"

Porscha was tired of her mother constantly pushing her own agenda. Maybe if she agreed to the one date, she could get Diane off her back. "I'm saying... I'm willing to go on a publicized date to take advantage of the extra publicity."

Her mother clapped her hands. "Excellent. I'll get the ball rolling with Ryan's people. You won't regret this."

Porscha didn't think so. Going on this date was a stopgap measure to distance herself from Xavier and prevent herself from falling in love with a man who wasn't the commitment type. She'd learned that about him the hard way three years ago when she thought they were on the relationship track and Xavier said they were friends and nothing more. She wouldn't make that mistake again.

The car stopped in front of the youth complex and a massive crowd was waiting *for her*. It was heady, because she had always dreamed of being here one day but had never thought about what came with the fame.

Stepping out of the vehicle, Porscha waved at fans. When a young girl called out for her autograph and handed her a marker, Porscha scribbled her name on the girl's T-shirt and walked quickly toward the front door.

Standing in the doorway was none other than Xavier Lockett.

And her heart stopped.

He looked magnificent in a blue denim shirt, dark denim jeans and white sneakers. His curls were neatly faded, and she loved how his groomed beard felt against her thighs when his face was buried between her legs.

Oh, yes, she was in deep with this man and that frightened her most of all.

Xavier sucked in a breath when Porscha's town car pulled up outside the complex. He tried not to stare when she strutted toward him in a chic white pantsuit and pointy, nude Christian Louboutin stilettos. Her lustrous hair was piled high in an intricate arrangement of curls, but it was her smile and the dimple in her right cheek that were her best features.

As Porscha moved toward him, Xavier found himself unable to look away. His pulse pounded as she came forward.

"Xavier."

"Ms. Childs, so great of you to be able to join us today."

Her eyebrow rose when he didn't use her first name, but she affected a smile. "I'm happy to be here."

"Thanks for coming. The children are so excited. Please follow me to the side entrance," Xavier led her to the gymnasium when he would have preferred to catch her hips and bring her closer so he could sweep his lips over hers. But it wasn't going to happen.

Her entourage was in pursuit behind them. He wasn't going to get any alone time with Porscha, but he had a special surprise for her later up his sleeve. He'd been in cahoots with Erin, and she'd helped clear Porscha's schedule so she would be his tonight and all day tomorrow until she had to head back to Los Angeles for filming on Sunday.

"Here we are," Xavier said, opening the side door and leading them to a green room. "If you can wait here, I'll come back for you. There's refreshment and light snacks."

Diane glanced down at the food he had laid out. "Porscha can't eat any of that. It's all carbs except maybe the fresh fruit."

Xavier nodded. "Noted. I'll see what else we have."

He knew Diane wasn't his biggest fan and he wasn't hers, either. He'd heard about women like her who used their children to get ahead, but he would never say that to Porscha. Diane was her mother after all. He was about to leave, when Porscha grabbed his arm. He found her looking up at him expectantly and he realized he hadn't said thank-you. "If I forget to say it, thank you for coming. You're doing me a huge favor."

She smiled. "You're welcome. I'll have to think of a way you can repay me."

"Oh, I have plenty of ways of showing my appreciation," Xavier whispered in her ear. Then he stroked her cheek with his palm and left the room.

It was hard to have a clear mind when Porscha was in the room. Xavier tended to lead with his libido instead of his head around her. He was thankful when he saw his mother gliding across the hall toward him with his father in tow. She looked regal in an all-white suit while his father wore his trademark pin-striped blue suit.

"Great work, my darling," his mother kissed Xavier's cheek. "What you've done here is nothing short of amazing."

"I have to agree with your mother on this one," Josiah said. "You knocked it out of the ballpark."

Earning his father's respect was a rare occurrence, so Xavier appreciated the attaboy. "Thanks, Dad."

"You ready to go out there and give your speech?" his father asked.

Xavier was more than ready and walked with his parents to the gymnasium, where the entire crowd was gathered—the youth who would use the sports complex, along with their families, the press and leaders in the community. Xavier noticed that Roman and Shantel, Julian and Elyse as well as Giana and Wynn were in the audience rooting him on.

Xavier headed to the podium. "I want to thank everyone for coming today. This project has been a labor of love not only for me, but for the Lockett Foundation. We want to be part of the fabric of our community and supporting the next generation of young talent, who need our help. They need uniforms and equipment, summer training camps and more, to reach their full potential. And this sports complex is my family's and the Atlanta Cougars' way of giving back."

"Why is this so important to you, Xavier?" one of the reporters shouted from the crowd.

"As many of you know, I had a short-lived career with the league, but before, I played in many high school and football arenas and stadiums around the state. I saw how desperate many of these teams were for basic necessities. I wanted other players to have the same resources I had. And now, with this complex, they'll have the facilities they need. But we won't stop there. Through the Lockett Foundation they'll get everything they need."

Xavier finished his speech. "We are excited to have a special guest here today to help kick off the grand opening of the complex. Please give a warm welcome to the one, the only, Porscha Childs!"

The crowd erupted in applause and Xavier turned and watched as Porscha came through the side entrance to the front of the room with a microphone in her hand.

"Hi, everyone." She waved. "I want to thank the

Lockett Foundation for inviting me to today's opening. Supporting our youth is near and dear to my heart. So would you like a song?"

"Yes!" The crowd cheered.

The melody from one of her most popular songs began playing and Xavier became enraptured as he listened to Porscha sing. He doubted he'd ever tire of hearing her voice.

After the song ended and the many congratulations from the kids, staff and his family, Xavier wanted to see only one person, but Porscha was nowhere to be found.

"Looking for someone in particular?" Giana inquired when Xavier peered beyond her through the dwindling crowd in the gymnasium.

Xavier returned his gaze to his sister. "Hmm…?" He just hoped Erin would live up to her end of the bargain and ensure Porscha arrived at their hideaway as planned.

"Well, you've answered my question as to who your secret lover is," Giana replied.

"Listen, Gigi." Xavier grabbed her arm and pulled her aside, away from the crowd.

"Don't backpedal now," Giana said, laughing. "Having her sing at my engagement party was one thing, but at the opening of our youth complex? C'mon, Xavier. You must think I don't have two eyes. I see the way you look at her."

"Is it that obvious?"

"Only to those who know you. Anyway, I was hoping to get to know Porscha, but she left in a flash."

"Don't get ahead of yourself, sis, we're just kicking it."

Giana raised a brow. "Ha, you can fool yourself if you want to, but no woman flies all the way across the country to sing a song for just a booty call. You mean something to her."

Hours later, when he arrived at their secret spot, Xavier wondered if Giana was right. Did Porscha care for him? He could admit Porscha was special to him. She didn't belong in his usual "love 'em and leave 'em" category. That was why he was unloading bags of groceries to make her dinner tonight. They were having their first official date.

When they'd been at the clinic, it was about leaning on each other for support both emotionally and physically. The last seven months were about sex, lots of it, and although he wouldn't trade a single second, tonight was about the two of them. And if Giana was right, Porscha would welcome seeing more from him. Xavier took the bags to the kitchen and immediately began laying out his game plan for dinner. He donned his apron and set to work.

An hour later, the candlelit table was set, and the meal was in the oven. Xavier didn't often cook, but there were a few dishes he'd mastered from his mother. One of which was shrimp and andouille sausage grits; he hoped Porscha liked it. He was putting the finishing touches on his butter-and-rum sauce for the bananas Foster when the alarm panel alerted him to the door opening.

She'd come.

Seconds later, Porscha walked into the kitchen in a crystal-encrusted corset top with black V-straps and a fringed miniskirt with Chanel ankle boots. "Wow!"

She glanced around at the dining room, from the muted candlelight to the elaborate dinner settings to the bucket of champagne chilling. "You did all this?"

Xavier shrugged. "Do you like it?"

"I *love* it!" Porscha rushed toward him and to his delight jumped into his arms, her svelte legs wrapped around his waist forcing Xavier to hold her pert bottom. She rewarded him with a long, luxurious kiss.

When they parted, they were both breathless. Xavier eased Porscha down to her feet, because as much as he'd have loved nothing better than to take her upstairs to the bedroom, tonight was about showing Porscha there was more to them than just sex. Though he intended to have a lot of *that* before the night was over.

"I can't believe you went to all this trouble," Porscha said. "No one has ever cooked for me."

"What about your mom?"

"Diane is terrible in the kitchen. She can't even cook eggs. It's how I got into bad eating habits, because we were always eating out."

"My mom comes from New Orleans, and cooking is in her blood. She made sure each of us had a few signature dishes in our repertoire. Shrimp and grits is my specialty."

"I can't wait to try it."

"Would you like some wine? I opened a bottle to breathe."

"Yes, please."

Xavier busied himself getting wineglasses from the sparsely furnished cupboard. Since it was a rental, only the basics were included, but it was enough for him to make Porscha a delicious meal. It was the first time they would focus on conversation rather than ripping each other's clothes off.

He poured them each a glass and led her over to the low sofas in the living room so they could talk.

"What was it like growing up in the Lockett household?" Porscha inquired, sipping her wine.

"Intense," Xavier responded, swirling the claret-colored liquid around in his glass so it left trickles running down the sides. "Roman was an athlete, much like myself, but it wasn't his passion. Instead, he followed our father around everywhere, learning everything he could so he could lead the Cougars someday. Then there was Julian. He always had his head in a book or was writing poetry, and my father hated it. He wanted him to be more like Roman, so they butted heads constantly."

"And Giana? How did she fit into all this machismo?"

"She was a tomboy, constantly trying to show our father she could do anything Roman could. She was desperate to be seen as something other than a weak female."

"Well, she's done that. Isn't she CEO of the Cougars?"

Xavier nodded. "That's right. And I'm darn proud of her. She proved everyone wrong, including our father, who thought all women should be barefoot, pregnant and in the kitchen."

Porscha cocked her head to one side. "And you?"

"I was born several years after the initial trio. At that point, my father had given up ever hoping for a son who would follow in his footsteps. You see, my dad played football in his youth, but was never quite good enough to make it in the big leagues. So he and his former business partner, Frank Robinson, purchased the Atlanta Cougars."

"I had no idea."

"Imagine his joy when I came along and loved football," Xavier replied. "He was at every youth football league game, but once he realized how good I was, it took a turn from doting father to drill sergeant. He constantly pushed me to practice. And losing, well, that wasn't allowed. *'There are only winners and losers in life, son,*—" Xavier imitated his father's deep baritone voice "—*and you are a winner,'* he'd always say."

"That was a lot of pressure to put on you at such a young age."

Xavier shrugged and took a slow mouthful of the dark red wine and swished it around before swallowing. "It was either excel or deal with the wrath of Josiah Lockett. I chose excellence."

"But then you were injured."

He nodded. "Suddenly, I wasn't the golden child anymore. I was a disappointment. A stain on the Lockett legacy."

Porscha reached for his hand. "You're not a stain, Xavier. You're an incredible man."

"Oh, don't go giving me praise. I'm no Boy Scout." When he'd been a quarterback, he'd been a notorious ladies' man with women lined up at his door, but the injury had brought him back to reality real quick. "The Xavier of three years ago had a big chip on his shoulder and thought he was God's gift to women."

"You've changed, right?" Porscha asked. "I think we all have the capacity for growth."

Xavier was glad she felt that way, because by the end of the night he was hoping she would see a way forward to them being more than bed buddies.

Porscha found herself relaxing as the evening progressed. They dined by candlelight and enjoyed the delicious meal Xavier had prepared. The shrimp, andouille sausage and grits were divine. She wished they could share more chill nights like this when she could let her hair down literally and figuratively. She rarely got the opportunity to do so. She was always *on* in case someone was photographing or filming her. She appreciated this respite.

"So," Porscha said, staring at Xavier intently from across the table while they enjoyed their dessert of bananas Foster. "Why dinner? Why all the romance?" She inclined her head to the candlelit table.

"Truth?"

She nodded. "That would be appreciated."

His gaze held hers. Porscha doubted she would tire of looking into his dark eyes rimmed with thick curling black lashes and well-defined brows. But it was his words that caught her by surprise. "We have no problem in the bedroom department, Porscha. We never have. We have a communication and trust issue. And tonight was about seeing if there's more to us than just sex."

Porscha was shocked by his words. She did want more than a sexual relationship with Xavier. She wanted the friendship and companionship they'd found those weeks at the clinic. She wanted to believe him, but she'd been burned before. Her experience with Gil and then her earlier disappointment over Xavier had scarred her. She wasn't sure if she could trust her own judgment again.

At the clinic, when she heard Xavier mention they were just friends and nothing more, it triggered flashbacks of Gil and her father. It made her feel worthless and unlovable. "I want to believe you, Xavier."

"Haven't I proven I can be trusted?" he asked. "All these months we've played completely by your rules, and I've gone along."

"Yes, you have." Xavier was as hungry for her as she was for him. She certainly hadn't experienced this strong an attraction with any other man. It was as if the memory of Xavier's lovemaking had haunted her the years they'd been apart.

"Maybe we could try dating and see where that leads. That's if you're willing to take a risk on me."

She wanted to, but she was afraid. She didn't want to get her heart broken again. It had taken too long to recover from their last affair. Xavier's reputation couldn't be forgotten, either. She had to stay in control of this situation. It had to be on her terms. Her rules.

"Let's take baby steps, okay?"

"If that's the way you want it."

"I do. And we can start with tonight."

Five

Xavier understood Porscha's reluctance. He'd made a mess of things between them before, and he knew his reputation as a playboy gave her pause. He would have to take it as a win that she wasn't saying no to dating altogether. It wasn't like he was ready to put a ring on it, but he wanted something more than a casual affair.

After clearing the table, they found themselves doing the mundane task of washing the dishes. He washed while she rinsed and put them in the drying rack.

"I can't remember the last time I did dishes," Porscha said. "I feel like I've been living out of a suitcase. The only time I haven't been was after the second album and my father's death."

Porscha rarely talked about that time in her life. Xavier knew it was a painful topic because she'd spiraled into a depression afterward. And it was exacerbated by the press because her sophomore effort hadn't lived up to the acclaim of her first one.

"You can talk to me about it," Xavier said as he finished up the last of the pots and pans and placed them on a drying mat on the counter.

Porscha paused, put down the drying towel and leaned against the counter to regard him. "My dad was my universe. Much like your father treats Giana, he treated me like a princess. But then he and my mom divorced when I was eight and suddenly my whole world was turned on its axis. He remarried. Started a new family, and I was persona non grata with the new wife."

"That had to be difficult." Xavier was fortunate his parents were still happily married and as much in love as they'd been the day they wed.

"It was. After the divorce, Mama became fixated on my talent. Before it had been sort of a hobby. I did a few singing competitions here and there. But then it all changed—instead of focusing on the heartbreak of losing my father, my mother poured all her time and energy into me and making sure I was a success. Voice and dance lessons. Rehearsals. Recitals. It was all an endless merry-go-round. Soon, I didn't even have time to see my father because we were always on the go chasing the dream."

"Do you think she was trying to keep you away from him?"

"Consciously? No. But it certainly felt that way at the time. It didn't help that I wasn't a fan of my stepmother's. I mean, she's the one who stole my father away. Needless to say, it caused a strain on our relationship, and he chose not to visit me and vice versa. I think my mother tried to overcompensate, so consequently I felt smothered. Over-mothered. Still do sometimes."

"Have you told her how you feel?"

"She gets defensive. Acts as if I don't love her or appreciate all she's done for me. But she doesn't get it, Xavier. I've sacrificed a lot, too. My entire childhood, *my life*, trying to fit the image of what *she* and the public want from me. It only became worse when Dad passed away. I went into a downward spiral of depression brought on by my guilt because I hadn't spent enough time with him, and the constant media scrutiny."

Xavier recalled seeing her picture splashed across the magazines and on social media. He hadn't known her then, but the press had been relentless.

"I stopped caring what I looked like. I ate one too many pints of Ben & Jerry's and gained a few pounds, but the press made it seem as if I was out of control. I helped them sell magazines, but it was hurtful. Here I am trying to deal with my own grief and being made a mockery of in the media. All the time, effort and hard work I put into my career was suddenly going down the drain. I had to get away. Get my head on straight. The clinic did that for me and it brought you to me."

"Come here." Xavier pulled her into his arms and hugged her tightly. He kissed the top of her head. "I'm glad you felt comfortable enough to share all of that with me."

"You bring me peace in the storm." She glanced up at him and Xavier got lost in her light brown gaze as she wrapped her arms around his waist. She felt warm and so damn good. Desire warred with an irritating wash of chivalry.

He'd brought Porscha here tonight to show her they could be more than bedmates. And he'd done that. She'd opened up to him and he wanted to protect her, but he couldn't deny his heart was pounding hard in his chest at having her so snug against him. She fit so perfectly. He wanted her.

Which was why he should pull away. She must have sensed his hesitance because she snaked her hand behind his neck and pulled him down to her. Her kiss was soft and gentle, yet unyielding. A thousand fireworks exploded inside his head as her lips opened beneath his.

"Porscha." He groaned her name as he reacquainted himself with her taste. She swayed in his arms, responding to his fervor. He couldn't help but touch her. His fingertips moved over her body, lingering at her waist. Skating upward to her hips. Cupping her buttocks and pulling her more firmly to him.

She gasped and it broke the spell. Xavier eased back and looked down at her. "I'm sorry. I didn't bring you here to seduce you, Porscha."

"I know." She smiled. "Now take me to bed."

"With pleasure." He picked her up in his arms and carried her to the bedroom.

Xavier kicked open the door and carefully laid Porscha down on the bed as if she were fragile. Then he gave her a long, leisurely kiss, which soon turned into something more, something deeper and more intense. They kissed until they were both gasping for air. Eventually, Xavier dragged his mouth from her lips to her throat. He could feel her pulse beating against his lips and felt himself growing hard.

He had to slow things down. He crouched down so he could unbuckle her impossibly high-heeled shoes and ease them off one at a time. When he began massaging her ankles and then her feet, Porscha moaned in ecstasy as if he was giving her the best orgasm she'd ever had.

He looked up at her. "Do you have any idea what you're doing to me when you make sounds like that?" He couldn't wait for her to make more when he made love to her. With an impatient tug, he pulled the straps of the corset free so he could lift it up and over her head. Then he was palming her breasts.

Porscha made a mewing sound like a cat, inciting him to kiss her again. He moved his lips over hers, teasing and coaxing a response from her until she parted her lips. Then his tongue slipped between them to dance with hers, but Porscha wasn't going to be an inactive participant.

"You have too many clothes on." She reached for the silk shirt he wore and pulled it out of his jeans. Then she began attacking each one of the buttons until one flew off. He gave a low laugh of pleasure at her impatience.

"Easy, love!" he teased.

"Don't easy me," she retorted. "I want you naked." She reached for the zipper of his jeans and before Xavier knew it, she was tugging them along with his briefs down his legs, allowing his erection to spring forward. When she took his length in her hand and began to stroke him with her palm, it was too much for him to handle.

He took back the power by kissing her and exploring her body, especially her tightly budded nipples. He anointed them with his tongue and grazed them with his teeth. Pleasure pulsed through every cell of his being. He couldn't wait to make her his, but he wanted to be sure she was ready. So he moved lower, blazing a trail to her stomach with his lips while simultaneously stroking his fingers up her legs.

She gasped when he peeled off her miniskirt and panties, especially when his fingers slicked into her honeyed heat. He moved them against her sensitive female flesh. She cried, she shook, and she shuddered. And when he couldn't take it any longer, Xavier moved away long enough to get a condom and tear the wrapper between his teeth. Her eyes widened as he smoothed it on. Then he positioned himself over her, lifted her bottom and entered her with one powerful movement. Pleasure exploded through him when her body gripped him, welcoming him in. He found himself retreating, then plunging again deep inside her tight, slick body.

Tingles shot up his spine as Porscha clutched his back, all the while entwining her smooth legs with his hair-roughened ones. She angled up to meet his feverish thrusts and Xavier's pulse raced with excitement. *This* was what he needed. He leaned forward to give her a soft kiss and she answered the call by teasing and cajoling his tongue with her own.

Porscha captivated his senses and Xavier wanted more. There was nothing cool or controlled about his movements. He began rhythmically thrusting harder and faster inside her. Desire ruled his brain, wiping out everything else. His hands cupped Porscha's bottom and moved her to accept him exactly the way he needed.

Their breaths began coming in short, sharp gasps. Porscha broke first and her body convulsed powerfully around his. Xavier heard her soft cries as he released a low, guttural groan, and his mind went blank as ecstasy in the purest form surged through him.

Porscha was barely aware of Xavier extricating himself to deal with the contraception. She felt turned inside out. Her hair was like rumpled silk across the pillows, but inside she was suffused with a sense of satisfaction that made her want to sleep for a thousand years.

Eventually, Xavier rejoined her in bed with a satisfied smile. "That was epic," he said, sliding between the covers.

She wished she understood what it was about him that she couldn't say no to. He seemed to know how to light up every single one of her nerve endings and make her body tremble at his touch. Even now, in the aftermath of their lovemaking, when her body should have been spent, she wanted him again. But she wasn't sure she could trust her feelings.

Had Xavier ever been in love? Because love was what she sought if their relationship was going to go any further. But they'd never discussed their past loves. She had no idea if there had ever been a woman who meant something to him, and she sure hadn't shared the terrible lapse in judgment she'd made with Gil.

It was embarrassing to talk about what a fool she'd been. Porscha was determined not to repeat her past mistakes. Time would tell if Xavier's intentions were real.

Six

As he drove to the Atlanta Cougars corporate head-quarters the following Monday, Xavier felt good about how the weekend had gone. Although he and Porscha had the best sex of his life Friday night, they didn't stay in bed on Saturday like they usually did most weekends. Instead, they'd gone for a long run on one of the running trails, with the paparazzi being none the wiser.

The press had no idea to look for Porscha in an upper-middle-class neighborhood in Atlanta. When they returned, they showered and spent the remainder of the day ordering pizza, eating popcorn and binge-watching Netflix. Eventually, they climbed into bed for another explosive lovemaking session that lasted well into the wee hours of the morning when Porscha finally sneaked away to head back to her place. Xavier felt like he'd proved to Porscha they had the makings of a relationship.

It was surprising to Xavier to want more than just a physical release: with other women he didn't *feel* anything other than pleasure. He didn't have to go deep because most of them only cared about his looks, his body or what being with him represented. Even though he wasn't a quarterback anymore, he was still part of the illustrious Lockett dynasty, and the ladies were eager to share in the glory.

But with Porscha he could be vulnerable. He'd shared with her what it was like growing up in the Lockett household. It wasn't easy when you fell from the top of the mountain in your father's eyes.

He was going to change the narrative. It was why he'd agreed to the mentorship program Giana suggested.

She'd emailed him info on a few players last week that she wanted him to meet with. There was last year's recruit, popular wide receiver Curtis Jackson. His father, Tim Jackson, was strict about the image his son presented. When Curtis got caught in a scandal last fall after trying to play hero, Julian's wife, Elyse, in her role as a publicist, had helped with the fallout. Consequently, Curtis was their most popular player. Then there was Wayne Brown, their new quarterback. Wayne was twenty-two and feeling himself. He was into the partying lifestyle and could soon find himself in a world of trouble if he wasn't careful. Xavier intended to have a serious chat with the young man.

Xavier pulled his Porsche convertible into one of the spots reserved for the Lockett family. Turning off the ignition, he hopped out and strode toward the door. Since he wanted to present a relaxed but professional image, he'd dressed in trousers and a navy button-down shirt. Instead of going toward the locker rooms or fitness center, he took the elevator to the executive suites and ran into Giana on the way.

"Xavier! I'm so happy to see you." Giana put her arm through his. "I have an office set up for you."

Xavier shook his head. "That's too much, Giana. I don't need one."

"Of course, you do." She walked him down the hall until they reached a door with his name on it. "I want you to feel part of the team. You're a Lockett after all. So let me do this for you, okay?"

"Fine." Xavier sighed and allowed her to walk him inside the office, which was decorated in cool blues and grays. He turned around. "It looks great. Now I want to meet the new players."

Xavier wasn't one for sitting on his butt. He was a man of action. Although he'd only played professionally for a few years, he'd parlayed that into sneaker and travel endorsements. Though some of those faded away after his injury, he'd invested well, and with his sportscaster salary, he wasn't hurting for cash.

"Okay, I can come with you." Giana started to follow him, but Xavier put a hand up.

"I don't need a babysitter." Xavier knew she meant well, but he didn't need his sister smothering him to death.

"Of course," Giana replied smoothly. "I'm here if you need me."

"Thanks." Xavier strode down the hall to the elevator bank. Within seconds, he was walking down corridors toward the weight room. He was sure to find the young men pumping iron because that was exactly where he would be—staying in tip-top shape for the new season. He ignored the ghosts of years past, but it was hard remembering how it felt to be running to the field in his uniform, helmet in hand.

Xavier blinked and reminded himself to focus on the future, because there was no turning back. But that didn't mean he wasn't affected. Football had meant *everything* to him. Had taken up his entire world until it was so narrow there was no room for anything else. He hadn't realized that until he'd come to care for Porscha. If he'd been a quarterback, he wouldn't have even considered wanting more from their relationship than sex.

The weight room wasn't crowded when he arrived. Wayne and Curtis along with a few other players were working out. Curtis was using the chest press while Wayne bench-lifted. They both glanced up when Xavier entered the room.

"Well, if isn't the legend." Wayne came toward him with his hand outstretched. Wayne was a charismatic young man with midnight-dark hair, blue eyes and an athletic physique made for being a quarterback.

"Xavier Lockett."

"Oh, I know who you are," Wayne responded with a large grin on his smooth brown face. "I've watched a lot of your film and I know I have big shoes to fill."

"You need only be your authentic self," Xavier replied. "The team hired you for a reason."

Wayne nodded. "I appreciate that. Thanks, man."

"You're welcome." Xavier glanced behind him toward the huskier young man behind him. "Curtis, good to see you." They'd met last year when his father brought Curtis to meet the Locketts prior to signing with the Atlanta Cougars.

"You, too, Mr. Lockett," Curtis replied.

Xavier laughed. "Just call me Xavier."

"Are you sure?"

"Absolutely," Xavier said. "I was hoping I could buy you both a smoothie and talk to you about the new mentorship program we're rolling out at the Atlanta Cougars. What do you say?"

"I presume you were off with the cad this weekend?" her mother asked when Porscha came down the stairs of her Pacific Palisades home on Monday morning in search of breakfast. She'd arrived late last night from Atlanta, while her mother and her team had come back here on Friday night.

Porscha rolled her eyes and went to the warmer on the counter near the stove and pulled out the spinach and mushroom omelet her personal chef had left for her. She wasn't about to get into an argument with her mother again about her and Xavier. She'd made her choice and Diane was going to have to live with it. After grabbing a fork from the drawer, she took her plate to the limestone countertop and began to enjoy her meal.

"You're not going to answer me?" Her mother huffed, putting her coffee mug on the counter. "Fine. Then I'll just tell you we leaked a photo of you from filming. You were looking adoringly at Ryan and now the entire world thinks you're an item."

"Is that really necessary?"

"Of course. It will heighten the public's interest."

Porscha sighed. "Well, that's what you wanted."

"It's what you wanted, too," her mother chided. "Ryan is one of the most popular actors in the world. Having your name linked with his would be a great boost to your career. Ryan's team were more than agreeable to the date."

Porscha wasn't excited by the idea of fake-dating Ryan. This weekend, her affair with Xavier had taken a turn. Xavier wanted more than just sex. He wanted them to date. But he hadn't indicated if they were going to be monogamous.

Did she even want that?

Maybe.

But she feared getting hurt again. Gil had a done a number on her head and her self-confidence. Porscha wasn't sure she could trust her feelings when it came to men. What was the harm in going out on a fake date with Ryan Mills? The exposure would help her career, but it would also allow her to keep some perspective where Xavier was concerned and see if she could trust him. Only time would tell.

"Xavier, thanks so much, dude," Curtis said, shaking his hand after their mentorship session ended in one of the many conference rooms at the Cougars' corporate headquarters. Xavier had already spoken with Wayne, and he'd left a short while ago. "I appreciate all your advice. It hasn't been easy navigating this new world of fame and fortune."

"From what I've seen so far," Xavier began, "you

have a rather good head on your shoulders. Your behavior last year, stepping in before that woman was assaulted at that hotel party, shows your character."

"I couldn't let that happen. Not on my watch."

"You did a good thing and I'm sure she appreciated it. Plus, it showed the media and any naysayers that you're exactly *who* you've represented yourself to be."

"I have my pops to thank for that," Curtis replied. "My father says selflessness, humility and truthfulness are the marks of an honorable man."

"Very well said. How would you feel about joining me in one of my charitable projects at the Lockett Foundation?"

"I'd like that." Curtis beamed. "I've been looking for the right vehicle to lend my name and support. Helping underprivileged youth means a lot to me."

They decided to meet up the following week. Xavier felt good about his first mentorship meetings. Giving advice about what he'd learned and the struggles he'd faced while playing professionally had been cathartic.

"So how did it go?" a deep tenor voice asked from behind him.

Xavier turned around and saw Roman standing in the doorway of the conference room. He smiled. "It went well. Actually, correct that, it went superbly."

"I'm glad." Roman came inside and closed the door. "I have to admit I was a bit worried when Giana made the suggestion. You haven't deigned to walk these hallowed halls since your injury."

"I needed to come back in my own time."

A wide grin spread across Roman's face. "Well, we

are happy to have you back in the fold. Care for some lunch? I had a cancellation."

"Sure, I'd like that." It had been too long since the two of them broke bread. During the season, Xavier was always on the air and sometimes traveling for work. And over the past year, Roman's entire life had changed. He'd gotten a wife and a baby all for the price of one.

They headed to the high-end restaurant on the top floor that was strictly for executives. Once they were seated, Xavier couldn't help but ask, "How's married life? Fatherhood?"

Roman had been a popular bachelor before he settled down. Xavier wondered how the transition was going, because Roman's wife, Shantel, had given birth to their son, Ethan Julian Lockett, late last fall.

"It's a lot," Roman grinned. "But I wouldn't change it for anything. Shantel is the love of my life and I'm lucky to have married her. Otherwise, who knows? She might have ended up with Julian."

"Good afternoon," the waiter interrupted them. Once he'd taken their order, they returned to their previous conversation.

Xavier laughed. "Really? How's that?"

"Oh, our brother had Shantel as his backup plan. Julian assumed Shantel would always be waiting in the wings if he ever tired of his playboy ways, but I beat him to the punch, and we fell head over heels in love, which is just as well because he wouldn't have met Elyse or be expecting his first child."

"Things happen the way they were meant to."

"True. And with Giana next in line for matrimony, that leaves you, baby brother, in Mama's crosshairs."

"I enjoy my life as it is," Xavier responded.

"And the woman you've been seeing on the side?" Roman inquired. "Don't think I've forgotten how Father mentioned her during our Christmas trip. Someone you don't want anyone to know about."

Xavier snorted. He was hoping Roman didn't recall the family holiday trip in which Josiah dropped the bomb that he knew Xavier's secrets. Their father hadn't named names, but he knew there was a woman in his life. "I was hoping you'd forgotten about that."

"Nah." Roman shook his head. "So, what gives? What's going on with you two?"

"It's nothing serious." Though this weekend had been different. They'd done a lot more talking than having sex. And after hitting the sheets, they'd cuddled and fell asleep.

"That's all?"

"Does there have to be more?" Xavier asked.

The waiter returned with Roman's Perrier and Xavier's Coke Zero.

"I don't know. That depends. How long have you been seeing each other?" Roman responded.

"Seven months, give or take."

"Sounds like a relationship to me."

Xavier denied it. "Porscha didn't want one. At least not at first. She was insistent we stay bed buddies, but nothing more. But she's willing to consider more now."

"Wait a minute." Roman glanced around to be sure no one was around and then looked back at Xavier. "Porscha? As in Porscha Childs who sang at Giana's engagement party last month? And sang at the youth complex?"

Oh, Lord. Xavier rolled his eyes upward. He had just put his foot in his mouth. He'd promised Porscha he'd keep their relationship private, but the cat was out of the bag now. "How else do you think someone as famous as Porscha would come to a private party?"

Roman shrugged. "I don't know. I assumed Giana with her connections arranged it. I had no idea you and Porscha were hooking up. How did that happen?"

"Denver."

"But that was nearly four years ago," Roman stated.

"We became friends while in therapy," Xavier replied. "And friends turned to lovers, but then I messed up. She heard me tell another patient we were friends and nothing else. She felt used and I didn't help matters because I was still reeling with the loss of my football career, and I said some less than flattering things."

"Then how did you reconnect?"

"Do you remember when Porscha sang the national anthem at the Atlanta Cougars game last year?"

"Yeah, I do. You've been together since then?" Roman asked.

Xavier nodded and sipped his drink. "At first, she was really angry with me and let me have it. The chemistry between us was still there. And the rest, as they say, is history."

Roman shook his head in disbelief. "And you've managed to keep this to yourself without saying a word? That's impressive."

"Her rules. Not mine," Xavier said tightly.

"And now? I sense you would like to change them?"

"I'm not saying I'm ready to jump the broom like the rest of you," Xavier responded, "but it doesn't have to be about sex all the time, either. I think I proved that to Porscha this weekend when I cooked for her, and we talked. I wanted her to know we didn't have to hit it and quit it every time we're together."

"Sounds like you want more, Xavier, but you're afraid to admit it."

Was Roman right?

Xavier certainly remembered what it had been like between him and Porscha at the clinic. Losing football had been like losing the part of himself that made him him, and Porscha had been a safe harbor in the midst of the chaos of his life. "I don't know. Maybe, but don't go inferring I'm ready to settle down."

"You might want to figure out what it is that you want."

"Why is that?"

"There are rumors circulating she's dating that famous actor Ryan Mills," Roman stated.

Xavier shook his head. "Nah, you're wrong. He's just the costar in her first film."

"Are you sure about that?"

He thought he was, but then again, he and Porscha weren't exclusive. Xavier had no idea if she was dating other men. Were the rumors true? If so, he would find out, because he wasn't about to give up. At least not yet. He would see how this played out, because one thing was for certain: there was no way Ryan Mills and Porscha could possibly have the fire between them that Xavier and Porscha had.

Seven

Porscha watched her reflection in the mirror as she executed the dance moves with the choreographer and her backup dancers. The song was fast and there were lots of intricate arm, leg and head movements that had to be sharp and crisp. They would all have to be in unison, because when they performed onstage for the BET Awards, she wanted the world to be amazed by their hard work. But she was tired, and it was only the middle of the week.

When they finished the rehearsal, Erin rushed over with a towel and bottle of water.

"Thanks." Porscha guzzled the drink.

"We have some of the couture outfits and high-heeled boots you're going to be using for the show,"

Rachel said, coming toward her. "We'll need you to start practicing in them."

Porscha nodded. Sometimes her career was exhausting, now especially. With the movie and soundtrack, Porscha was going to be everywhere, which left little time for herself. Now that the choreography session was over, it was off to the film set because she had to refilm a scene with Ryan that the director hadn't liked when they filmed the day prior.

Porscha was anxious. Both of their teams had gotten together and agreed they would have a date on Saturday night. They would hit one of the popular celebrity spots for dinner, followed by an appearance at a nightclub where the entire VIP area would be roped off for them. From a professional standpoint, the date was a no-brainer. The buzz from their date would keep everyone talking. But personally, Porscha was starting to wonder if she'd made the right decision in agreeing.

She and Xavier had had such a great weekend. He'd cooked for her and openly discussed his family life, and she'd seen another side to him. The softer side she'd discovered when they were in Denver. Perhaps they could be more to each other? Except she had a bad case of stage fright after her experience with Gil.

Am I projecting my fears and past hurt onto our relationship? She hadn't yet told Xavier about this date but maybe she should. No matter how much distance she wanted to keep to prevent herself from falling for Xavier, she didn't feel good about keeping the date with Ryan from him. She had to tell him.

Porscha left the dance studio and headed to the car waiting to take her to the film set. A crowd of fans along with the paparazzi were gathered outside. A few lobbed questions at her.

"Is it true about you and Ryan?"

"Are you secret lovers?"

Porscha chuckled to herself as she slid inside the vehicle. *If they only knew.* Erin and her mother soon followed, and Jose was the last to hop into the passenger seat next to the driver.

"You were right," Porscha said once the car was on the move. "The rumor mills are as active as ever."

"They are," her mother said from beside her. "I've already had requests from *People* and *In Touch* hoping to get an interview with you both about your love story."

"Ha!" Porscha snorted. "Like that's going to happen. I don't mind going along with the ruse of a public date to benefit both our careers, but I'm not going to outright lie." Although she and Xavier weren't monogamous, Porscha was already regretting her decision.

"All right, all right," her mother replied. "I was merely telling you your options. You don't have to bite my head off."

Was she? She and her mother hadn't always had a contentious relationship. Once upon a time, Porscha had wanted to be like Diane, but after her father left them, her mother had changed. She'd become hard and brittle. The hugs and soft words had gone away and she had transformed into a taskmaster constantly pushing Porscha to succeed. But she did love her. "I'm sorry, Mom."

Diane glared at her. "Are you, Porscha? You take

for granted everything I do for you. I only want the best for you."

She hated when her mom acted put-upon, because Porscha's success gave her mother an extremely comfortable lifestyle.

"Dating a man I barely know hardly qualifies as wanting the best for me," Porscha replied and turned to stare out of the window at the Los Angeles skyline as they whizzed by on the freeway.

They spent the rest of the journey in silence and when they arrived, Porscha hopped out as soon as Jose opened the door. She rushed to her trailer and once there, shut and locked the door. She needed some time to herself, which she rarely got. There were always people milling around and sometimes there was no space to breathe. She could feel herself becoming anxious.

Porscha tried the breathing technique the therapist at the clinic had taught her to use when she felt her world spinning out of control. It didn't work. Instead, she pulled out her phone and called Xavier.

She was afraid of needing anyone. Self-reliance and self-confidence had been a big part of her recovery and she was proud of herself, but there were times it would be nice to be held. And when she was in Xavier's arms, she felt safe and protected.

He answered after several rings. "Hey, what's up?"

His voice sounded weird, strained even. "Is everything okay?" She'd been calling him to boost her spirits, but something was off.

"I'm fine."

Her intuition told her something was up. Xavier was

usually more talkative when she called. Had he heard about her and Ryan?

"Listen, Xavier, I need to tell you something."

"Let me guess—you're dating Ryan Mills?" Xavier offered.

Porscha nearly dropped her phone. "You know?"

"I'd have to be in a cave not to," Xavier said. "I have a phone."

She heard the sarcasm in his tone.

"The date means nothing." Porscha hated saying it because it was exactly the words Xavier had used to describe their relationship once upon a time. "It's just business."

"If it were nothing you would have told me," Xavier responded hotly.

A knocked sounded on her trailer door. "Porscha, we need you on set in ten minutes."

She glanced down at her Cartier. "I'm sorry, Xavier, I have to go. I need to shower and get on set. Can we talk later?"

"If you can find the time." His response was curt and then he ended their call.

Porscha stared down at her phone. Had he just hung up on her? He was pissed that she hadn't told him about Ryan and he had every right to be. She should have told him about the arrangement. Maybe she hadn't because she was afraid of getting too close to Xavier. But now, thanks to her keeping secrets, she'd gotten her wish and put distance between them.

Xavier was furious with Porscha. How long had she been planning to keep the date with Ryan from him?

If he hadn't confronted her, how long would she have kept up the ruse? He would have to think about it later, though; he had his own issues to deal with. He was meeting his agent, Jevon Butler, for happy hour. Jevon had been insistent Xavier take the meeting because he had *big* news.

He was ambivalent about his on-air career. Being a sportscaster was the last thing on his mind when he'd been sitting in that Denver clinic, but then his father had called him during the end of his stay to tell him he'd gotten him a sweet deal with ASN, one of the big sports networks in Atlanta.

Xavier would have rather taken some time to get his head on straight. Instead, mere months after his knee injury, he'd been seated in front of a camera talking *about* football. He should have put his foot down, but who could say no to Josiah Lockett?

Jevon was waiting for him at a table outside, wearing a slim-fitting, ruthlessly tailored suit. His dark waves were combed back from his face and he had a hint of a tan. He rose when Xavier approached. "Good to see you, my friend. What can I get you to drink?" He motioned a waiter over.

"A Scotch, if you don't mind."

"I'll get it started for you," the waiter said and left them alone.

"So?" Xavier quirked a brow. "What's the big news?"

"Shelby Mitchell, the top sports anchor at ASN, is taking a leave of absence to deal with some personal matters, so the league is looking for someone to replace him."

"What does that have to do with me?"

"Duh," Jevon said. "They are looking at you, Xavier. In you, they see a good-looking former quarterback who knows his stuff. You've got loads of charisma on camera, and by having you in the seat they could reach millions in the younger demographic."

"I don't know, Jevon. I was going to tell you that I was considering stepping away from the camera and doing something more fulfilling with my life."

"C'mon, X. As one of the top anchors for ASN, you would have an even bigger platform to support the charities you love and bring in even more money."

"It's not just about the money," Xavier said. Since losing football, he'd been trying to find his purpose, and the charities brought him joy.

"You're honestly willing to turn down this gig and give it to someone else?"

"If they are more passionate about it than I am, yes," Xavier said. "I'm still quite wealthy because I was smart with my income early on in my career and with my endorsements." Even though those had soon dried up once the companies realized he no longer had a football in his hand.

Jevon sighed. "I didn't realize you'd gone soft on me, Xavier. I thought you would jump at the chance. It's a high-profile position. A lot of eyes would be on you and every lady would certainly want to know you."

High-profile.

Xavier's ears perked up at the term. He hadn't thought about it like that. If he were to consider taking on the role, he would be making his current seven-figure salary several times over. Maybe then Porscha would be willing to explore the possibility of dating him exclusively, and *publicly*.

"All right, I'll consider it."

A large smile spread across Jevon's angular face. "Oh, thank God. I was beginning to think you'd lost the fire in your belly to prove you were back on top."

"Oh, I'm back!" Xavier stated.

Now he had to show Porscha he was just as big a star as Ryan to be seen on her arm.

"Don't be nervous, darling," her mother stated from Porscha's bedroom at her Palisades home on Saturday evening. Rachel had made the final touches on her outfit for the evening, which was a low V-cut crop top with a large pendant necklace, accompanied by a slim-fitting miniskirt, a gold-chained belt and killer Manolo Blahnik heels.

"Your abs look amazing," Rachel said, adjusting the chain on the skirt, "but I do think the top needs a little something." She returned several minutes later and placed two silicon breast enhancer pads into her bra. "There, that's better. Now that gives you some cleavage and accents the pendant necklace."

Then there was Kristen, her personal double threat because she could do hair and makeup. She'd put Porscha's hair in a messy but glam updo and accentuated her eyes with smoky makeup, a bold swipe of red lipstick and a red manicure that showed off a chunky gold ring.

"Thank you, Kristen." Porscha stepped away from all the pampering to look at herself in the mirror. At least no one could fault her look. Her image was exactly what her label and her team wanted her to project.

Sex.

Sex sells, but it wasn't who Porscha was underneath. It was all a mirage. She would rather wear a pair of comfy sweats like she'd done nearly every day in Denver. Her life had been simpler then, but then she'd gone there to escape her grief and failing career.

Was she doing the right thing going out with Ryan?

"You ready?" her mother asked, coming up behind Porscha and looking at her through the mirror. "The car is ready."

Porscha spun around. "I don't know if I can do this. If I *should* do this."

"Clear the room," her mother ordered.

Everyone was used to Diane's brusque tone and quickly exited Porscha's bedroom. Once the door was closed, her mother grabbed her by the shoulders. "What are you doing, Porscha? Do you have any idea how serious this is?"

"Of course, I do, Mama," Porscha said, spinning away and out of her grasp. "Because you won't let me forget it."

"Then you *know* the ball is already in motion and we can't change the tide of events tonight. We worked this out with Ryan's team. He's expecting you. To not show up would *ruin* you. Do you hear me?"

"Yes," Porscha said through clenched teeth.

"Then go do your job."

"Fine, but know this." She pointed at her mother. "Just because you and Ryan's team have concocted this elaborate ruse for publicity doesn't mean I have to buy into it."

Porscha turned on her heel and left the room. Erin was waiting for her outside the door. "Are you okay?" she asked, searching Porscha's face. "Diane is in a real mood."

"I'm fine," Porscha responded. She'd gotten herself into this mess, so she would have to get herself out of it. Gingerly, she walked to the end of the hall, down the staircase and outside in the spiky heels Rachel had chosen. Jose was waiting for her and helped her into the car.

At least in the Bentley, on the way to meet Ryan, she was blessedly alone with her thoughts. She opened her crystal-studded Jimmy Choo satin purse and found her phone. She wanted to call Xavier back and explain, tell him the date was business. Surely once she clarified it was for publicity, he would understand. It wasn't as if she'd betrayed him. And there was no ring on her finger. No commitment between them that they couldn't see other people.

But she never had.

Until now.

And as far as she knew, neither had Xavier.

Since they'd been together, Xavier hadn't been photographed on social media with other women like he'd done after their breakup almost four years ago. Did that mean he was exclusively seeing her? Or should she say exclusively *sleeping* with her? They'd never set those parameters and she certainly hadn't mentioned it this weekend because she hadn't wanted to seem needy or desperate.

When the date was over, Porscha would call Xavier, clarify her arrangement with Ryan and make things right between them. It wasn't like their relationship was over. They'd just hit a minor bump, but they could fix it, right?

Eight

"Deal 'em." Xavier ordered. He, Julian, Roman, Wynn and Silas Tucker, Wynn's friend, were spending a rare Saturday night together at Roman's house because the wives had decided to go to some fashion show with Angelique Lockett, leaving the men to their own devices.

"Bossy much?" Julian asked with a smirk as he continued shuffling the cards. "Don't forget you're the baby in this family and we—" he glanced at Roman across the table "—are your big brothers. You need to show us some respect, otherwise we'll have to show you who's boss and take all your money."

"And you think that's you?" Xavier laughed and then tipped his beer back for a swig. "You do realize I have about twenty pounds and four inches on you."

Julian shrugged. "Size doesn't matter. Just because you knuckleheads got Dad's height means nothing. I got Mom's eyes." He pointed at his face. "Trust me when I say the ladies, including my wife, have no problem with this package."

Roman burst out laughing, spitting out some of his beer. "Julian, you're a ham. You know that?" He reached for a napkin and dabbed his face.

"We're playing poker. We're supposed to trash-talk," Julian retorted evenly. Then he dealt one card facedown to each of them and then went around the table again to deal another four cards until they all had five.

"So we're playing five-card draw?" Wynn asked.

"Yeah, anyone got a problem with that?" Julian snapped.

"Nah, just want to know. Because when I wipe the floor with you, you won't see it coming," Wynn countered.

"I love all the trash talk," remarked Silas, who was a celebrity chef with a slew of restaurants and television shows. His wife, Janelle, was the hottest supermodel around. They'd recently reunited after a long separation.

"You're all playing with the king of poker," Xavier announced, joining the fray. "Back in the day, when I was on the road with some of my teammates we would play until the break of dawn, or until the bets were so outrageous you finally gave up."

"You think you can best me?" Roman asked. "Good luck."

Their banter continued late into the evening. They

laughed, talked, drank beer and ate pizza. Eventually the betting was in the thousands, and Xavier knew he had his brothers on the ropes. Both had to replace or discard dozens of cards, but Xavier had become quite adept at card counting. He was going in for the kill, but then his phone pinged.

Glancing down, he saw it was an alert about Porscha. He'd put them on his phone months ago. Whenever she was mentioned in the press, Xavier wanted to know, in case she needed him or he could help with any fallout. She hadn't asked him to, but he remembered the anxiety and depression she'd experienced from the negative media attention.

However, he was angry when he opened his Instagram app.

America's Next Super Couple: Ryan and Porscha!

"Damn!" Xavier didn't realize he'd said it out loud until he felt Roman and Julian coming behind him to glance at his phone.

"Why do you care who Porscha Childs is dating?" Julian asked. He walked to the refrigerator, pulled out another beer, unscrewed the cap and began to drink.

"Since he's been tapping that for months," Roman replied.

Xavier glared at him. "Do you have to be so crass?"

"My apologies," Roman responded. "Our dear brother has been sleeping with the songstress since last year."

"Wow!" Wynn said, shocked. "Is that why she sang at our engagement party?"

Xavier shrugged. "She wanted to keep it a secret."

"And why am I the last to know?" Julian came toward Xavier and thumped him on the chest with his middle finger.

"Because it wasn't exactly open for discussion," Xavier replied. "I mentioned her completely by accident to Roman and had to spill the beans, but that's beside the point. Porscha is out on a date with Ryan Mills, Sexiest Man Alive. How can I compete with that?"

"You can't," Julian said.

"Julian, do you have to be so blunt?" Roman asked.

"Don't get in your head," Silas interjected. "It's tough having a wife in the public eye. I know. Janelle and I were estranged for five years. I had no idea who she was messing with while she was living the supermodel lifestyle, but at the end of the day, we were able to come back from it. You can, too."

"That's all fine and good, Silas," Julian said. "But Xavier can only be who he is and if that's not good enough for her, then Porscha Childs is not the one for him."

Xavier shook his head. "You don't understand."

"Yes, I do," Julian stated hotly. "You have feelings for her and it's like a kick in the gut to imagine your lady with another man."

"Yeah, but she waited until the absolute last minute to try and tell me, and even then I had to help her out," Xavier replied. "And all she said was its business and she'll call me later."

"And what would you have done if she told you earlier?" Roman inquired. "Asked her not to go?"

"Of course."

"Then you're going to have come clean with Porscha and tell her what you want. Do you know that?" Roman asked.

Xavier shook his head. He wasn't sure what he wanted from Porscha. All he knew was that he didn't want their relationship to revolve purely around the bedroom. But what did he want it to be? Boyfriend-girlfriend? Their relationship had never been clarified because Porscha wasn't sure she could trust him. So instead, she'd gone out with another man. It burned Xavier.

"I suggest you figure it out before you talk to Porscha," Julian replied. "Because if you're asking her not to date other men, you better be offering her something else in return."

"I don't want marriage."

"Then what? Dating? Exclusivity?" Roman asked. "Figure it out, Xavier."

After he left Roman's, Xavier headed home to the guesthouse. To afford himself some privacy, he'd moved in, and he was glad he had. He wouldn't want to face his parents—his mother in particular, with all her questions. Because she would know instantly he was upset.

And he was.

To arrange a date of this magnitude took planning—Porscha had to have known about it for a while, but she'd kept it from him. He was mad and jealous. Jealous that another man was spending time with Porscha. Those moments were his and no one else's.

Damn her!

Julian was right.

He was starting to have feelings for Porscha, and he needed to figure out what to do next.

"You look fantastic," Ryan told Porscha at dinner that evening. She'd arrived at the restaurant with much fanfare to find the press in high occupancy. Crowds were screaming her name and holding up pictures of her and Ryan together, saying they'd make beautiful babies.

The whole situation was out of control.

But Porscha did her part and stopped for photos, waving at all the fans and press before heading inside. Ryan was already waiting for her at their table. He rose when she walked up and pulled out her chair. She wondered if he was always chivalrous or whether it was for show, because all eyes in the restaurant were on them.

"Thank you. You aren't too bad yourself," she offered. It was the best she could do. Ryan was handsome and slim, but he was several inches shorter than Xavier. Xavier was tall with a broad chest and powerful shoulders, and had a commanding presence.

"I'm glad our people set this up," Ryan said, sitting back in his chair to regard her. "I've always been a huge fan of your work."

"Really?"

"Oh, yeah, your first album was amazing and this last one, *Metamorphosis*, was pure genius."

Porscha laughed. "Has anyone told you you're good at stroking egos?"

Ryan shrugged. "It's a gift."

"If we're passing around compliments, then I have to tell you your last film was epic. I really think you should have won the Oscar." Ryan had been nominated but hadn't won, even though he'd picked up statues at the Golden Globes and Screen Actors Guild Awards.

"I've come to accept Academy voters don't get me," Ryan replied, reaching for his wineglass and taking a sip. "But that's not going to stop me from trying."

"That's admirable. And I understand. When you fall, you still have to get back up," Porscha replied.

Ryan nodded. "I assume you're referring to your second album?"

"Yes." And that was all Porcha was going to say on the topic. She wasn't about to share confidences with Ryan, a man she hardly knew.

Ryan must've gotten the hint, because he moved on to a different topic. He opened a bottle of champagne and they toasted to the evening. Then he began discussing their movie. What he felt was going wrong and what could use improvement, but all Porscha could think about was Xavier. He was upset she hadn't confided in him, the one she normally shared her secrets with. Surely, she could smooth the waters with Xavier. She was dying to know. After dinner, while the waiter went to get their dessert, which she had no intention of eating, Porscha rushed to the ladies' room to powder her nose. The real reason was to check her phone. When she did, she went to a stall and closed the door. Unclasping her purse, she glanced down at her phone. There was a text from Xavier.

Hope you're enjoying your date with the Sexiest Man Alive.

He'd obviously meant it to be sarcastic, but it had the opposite effect, because Porscha went from feeling guilty to anger. How dare Xavier stand in judgment of her? It wasn't like they'd made promises. They never discussed next month, let alone next year. Up until this weekend, he was keen for sex and had agreed to the no-strings fling.

He had asked her to consider them becoming more than bedmates, but she hadn't agreed. She wanted to take baby steps because she was protecting her heart and shielding herself against getting hurt. And she'd done that, but had she also kept Xavier at arm's length?

The text told her he was bothered. She wanted to call him and tell him the date was a media ploy, but she couldn't. Not here in the bathroom of one of the most notorious celebrity restaurants. Her conversation could be overheard and spread on every press outlet before she made it back to her table. She would have to deal with Xavier in private.

Porscha returned to the table and Ryan rewarded her with the movie-star smile he was known for. "I hope you don't mind, but I took the liberty of telling the waiter dessert wasn't needed."

Porscha smiled. "Thank you. Carbs and sugar are a no-no for me."

"Completely understand. Are you ready to go? I believe our team arranged a nightclub appearance. My car is just outside."

Porscha nodded. Her mouth was as dry as the Sahara Desert. Once she walked out those doors with Ryan, they would be photographed together. Add that to the pictures people had snuck of them at the dinner table;

she had caught a few fellow diners pulling out their phones when they thought she wasn't looking. Xavier would see it all.

"Yes, of course." She rose to her feet and Ryan, ever the gentleman, pulled out her chair. He placed his hand on the small of her back and led her out of the restaurant. Porscha hated that. She wanted Xavier's hands on her, not his, but she feigned happiness especially when they walked outside.

They were greeted by a large mob of reporters that had doubled in size from her earlier entrance. They all were yelling and throwing questions out at them. She and Ryan paused at the door of the dark Escalade idling at the curb and posed for pictures, which Porscha knew would run on every entertainment show, social media outlet and blog. She waved one final time before climbing inside and braced herself for what was to come.

Because there would be a price to pay for this escapade.

The end of her affair with Xavier.

Nine

Xavier didn't usually box. He much preferred the weight room at the family home gym, but today was another story. He was hitting the punching bag with all the force of a Mack Truck. He was so angry that he could spit nails. He'd called Roman and Julian to join him, but they were otherwise occupied, so his soon-to-be brother-in-law, Wynn, would do in a pinch.

The two men had come to an easy alliance after Giana had gotten engaged to Wynn. Xavier was often at their home for dinner or just to play pool, but today, Xavier needed to blow off some steam. He'd seethed when his phone kept beeping with photos of Porscha and Ryan on a night out on the town. Eventually, he'd turned off the damn notifications, but that had done nothing to calm him. He was still furious with the little minx for gallivanting around town with another man while he couldn't stop thinking about her.

"Easy, man," Wynn said, walking up to Xavier as he pummeled the punching bag. "That bag did nothing to you."

Xavier stopped to glare at Wynn. Wynn had an athletic and lean build from all the running he did. He had a tawny, light brown complexion and a perpetual five-o'clock shadow. "Ouch. Did I do something to offend you?" Wynn asked.

He shook his head. "It's not you, Wynn. It's me. I'm angry that I let someone get under my skin when I shouldn't have."

Wynn placed the gym bag he came with on the floor. "Care to talk about it?"

"Not now. Get changed and meet me in the boxing ring."

"All right. Give me a few," Wynn replied and rushed off to the locker room.

Xavier reminded himself Wynn wasn't the enemy. He was a sounding board. When he returned several minutes later, Xavier had gotten himself under control and was already in the ring wrapping his hands.

Wynn was dressed in a T-shirt and shorts and holding his gloves and mouth guard. He jumped up, lifted the ropes and entered the ring. "So, you ready to tell me what's got you hot and bothered?"

"Let's spar first," Xavier said, putting on his gloves and guard.

"All right, this is your funeral," Wynn replied with a smirk. "I'm pretty good at this."

Xavier didn't mind. He was more than up to the challenge.

They sparred for nearly an hour, with Xavier giving as good as he got. Wynn wasn't lying when he said he was excellent. Xavier managed a few jabs to catch him off guard while Wynn nearly knocked Xavier down a few times, but Xavier righted himself quickly.

He probably wasn't in the right head space to be here, but he needed something to burn off some tension, and boxing did that. Eventually, they called it quits and took off their gloves.

"Good match, Xavier," Wynn said, wiping his face with the towel he'd left on the ropes. "If I didn't know any better, I would think you sparred all the time."

"I don't do it often enough, but I know my way around," Xavier responded, wiping his face with the bottom of his tank top.

"I can see that. So, what did you want to talk about?" Wynn headed over to the water station and poured them both cups of water. He handed one to Xavier, which he quickly drank.

"Women."

Wynn laughed. "Why am I not surprised? It's true what they say that men are from Mars and women are from Venus, because we see things differently. Are you still upset about Porscha? If I recall from our convo last night, you guys never outlined exclusivity."

"Don't you think I know that?" Xavier responded hotly. "It's why I'm so upset." He stood up and began pacing the floor. "I guess I assumed that was a given." At Wynn's look of incredulity, he continued, "And yeah, I get that was a bonehead move. I just never thought she'd be looking somewhere else, especially not a famous movie star."

"You feel like you can't compete?"

"Of course, I can't," Xavier returned. "I can get any woman I want, but sometimes I doubt myself. I look in the mirror and see a washed-up former quarterback with a knee injury. I want the glory I had before."

"You might not be tossing a football around every Sunday, but you picked yourself up, dusted yourself off and found a new career. Second, what you've done with the Lockett Foundation is nothing short of kick-ass. I was just telling Giana that my company is going to donate."

"You don't have to say that, Wynn."

"I'm not saying it because I'm about to be your brother-in-law. I'm a businessman. Do you have any idea how many charities come to me for a donation? But I only choose those I have a real connection to and your work with underprivileged youth speaks to me. I don't know if you knew, but Silas and I grew up using the Boys & Girls Clubs services. So trust me when I say this, you're doing magnificent work."

Xavier had heard about Wynn and his celebrity chef friend's ties to the organization. "Thanks, bro. I appreciate it." Wynn's words meant a lot. Xavier couldn't let the past continue to rule him, but that was easier said than done.

"Ryan Mills is just a pretty face after all," Wynn responded.

Both men laughed.

"That may be so, but Porscha didn't tell me until the

very last minute and didn't give me any details. That sticks in my craw."

"Then tell her. Keep it one hundred."

Wynn had a point. He was going to tell Porscha exactly how he felt about her rendezvous with America's favorite actor. And afterward, he would decide how to proceed with their current arrangement.

"You killed it last night, darling," her mother told Porscha the next morning while she lounged in her bed. "I've brought you some hot tea." She placed the teacup and saucer on the nightstand beside Porscha's bed.

"Thanks." Porscha pushed herself into the upright position and placed several pillows behind her so she could drink the tea. "What are they saying?"

"That you and Ryan are the next supercouple. The movie is going to be smashing. How great you look together. It's all positive," her mother replied, sitting on the edge of the bed.

Porscha sipped her tea. "Good."

"Good?" Her mother's expression showed her disappointment. "That's all you have to say?"

"What do you expect, Mama? An attagirl?" Porscha asked.

"I don't expect to be mocked, Porscha. I would think you would be happy to have all the positive press. We changed your narrative. People no longer remember the sullen, depressed and overweight Porscha. All they can see is a happy, fit and successful singer and actress."

Was that all she was? Porscha wondered. Like she wasn't a human being with feelings and emotions? Well, she had them. Just because she tried to fit the mold everyone expected of her, it didn't mean she was a robot.

"Can you please go? I'm tired."

"I thought perhaps we could do something fun together."

"Not today." It was one of her rare free days with nothing on the calendar and she wanted to lie in bed and mope. Mope because Xavier hadn't answered a single one of her calls or texts.

At first, she'd thought about ignoring his sarcastic congratulations. And she'd done a good job of it. Going with Ryan to the club had kept her mind off Xavier. But once there, she'd had a challenging time faking interest in Ryan when all she wanted to do was clear the air with Xavier. In the end, the date had limped along until eventually Ryan brought her home. When he'd gone in for a kiss, it landed on Porscha's cheek, and she bade him good-night, much to his consternation.

"If that's what you want…" Her mother's voice trailed off as if she was expecting a different answer, but Porscha didn't change her mind. She wanted to be alone.

Once the door closed, Porscha fell back against her pillows. She understood Xavier was upset. She hadn't told him in advance about the date and once she did, she had to rush off the phone. But they'd never set the parameters of their relationship. If he wanted more, if he wanted exclusivity, then he would have to tell her. She wasn't a mind reader.

The week whizzed by. Xavier met up with Curtis and discussed partnering with the Lockett Foundation on their inner-city youth programs. He also completed the interview with De'Sean Jones that Vincent had requested. Vincent was right: with his background and player insight, the interview went great. The network was happy and, consequently, the job as top anchor of ASN was within his grasp. Jevon was still negotiating the particulars of the agreement, but soon Xavier would be in the driver's seat. And this time, he'd done it on his own, with no help from his father. In no time, he would be a household name among sports enthusiasts and Porscha would be proud to have him on her arm.

Xavier tried not to let it bother him that the media were saying Porscha and Ryan were an item. Their date was splashed all over the internet, social media, everywhere he turned. He couldn't escape them. And nothing he seemed to do took his mind off the fact that the woman he'd been having an affair with was creeping out with another man. It was made harder by her repeated calls and texts, which had stopped a few days ago after he refused to answer them.

The shoe really was on the other foot. He wasn't used to being in the *wronged* position. Usually, he was the playboy wronging unsuspecting females, but in this case, Porscha was the player. It wasn't enough that he was in her bed. She craved the fortune and fame that came from being with someone as wildly popular as Ryan Mills.

As a quarterback, Xavier had had his share of dates, but there was something about movie stars, like the Idris Elbas, Michael Ealys and Morris Chestnuts of the world, that women seemed to love. A sportscaster wasn't sexy to all the ladies, but his name in Atlanta went far.

Maybe that was what he needed. To get back on the horse and get his groove back. Women did it all the time. He was Xavier Lockett after all. He wasn't going to sit and whine about Porscha keeping her options open; he would do the same.

He called up his former teammate, Allen Lewis, a known womanizer, and arranged to meet him on Saturday night. Why not? He was single and ready to mingle.

Saturday came quick and Xavier needed the distraction. He donned black slacks and his favorite purple silk shirt and met up with Allen at a new restaurant that was all the rage. He knew it was juvenile of him to go tit for tat with Porscha, but he wasn't about to sit home and worry about what she was up to.

"Xavier, my man." Allen gave him a quick hug when Xavier found him and several of his compadres in the VIP area of the restaurant. "Can't believe we managed to get you out on a Saturday night. We all figured you were booed up and some woman had her legs wrapped tight around you."

A few of the other men laughed, but Xavier frowned. He didn't appreciate being the butt of anyone's jokes. "No one rules me," Xavier said curtly.

"Glad to hear it," Allen said. "Should we get you a bourbon or a Scotch? I can't remember your poison."

"A Scotch will be fine," Xavier said through tight lips. He'd forgotten how annoying Allen could be.

After Allen signaled the waiter and ordered his drink, he returned to the group. He bumped shoulders with Xavier. "Did you catch those gorgeous ladies that just walked in?"

It was hard not to, Xavier thought, glancing at the trio of beauties sauntering past them. One was a platinum blonde wearing the tiniest dress he'd ever seen; it might as well be a shirt. There was a leggy brunette in a fire-engine red catsuit with the zipper low enough to see her bountiful breasts. Rounding out the trio was a stunning Latina with a high ponytail, in a skintight, hot-pink dress that didn't leave much to the imagination.

They were there to be noticed, and every man in the room did, including Xavier. He was tired of chasing women, but he didn't have to wait long. Once the women set eyes on their group and recognized some of the Atlanta Cougars players, they quickly made their way over, introducing themselves as Dawn, Skylar and Marissa.

The Latina named Marissa came over to Xavier. "I don't think I know you."

"Do you want to?" Xavier inquired.

Marissa smiled. "A tall drink of water like you, heck yeah."

And that was how Xavier's night went, from hanging with the boys to having a bevy of beauties at their side. Conversation was banal at best, but Xavier refused to leave early. If nothing else, he had something to prove to himself—that he was still *the man* and no female, Porscha included, could break him.

Marissa was extremely willing to laugh at his jokes, and that worked for Xavier. He needed a boost of confidence.

Eventually, the night moved from the restaurant to a men's club in town. The drinks flowed among the group until everyone began coupling up, by the end of the evening. Marissa stayed by Xavier's side, and he hadn't minded it, but when it was time to go, Xavier knew he was going home *alone*. As much as he'd enjoyed the night out with the fellas, he did miss being with one woman.

And she wasn't just any woman.

She was Porscha Childs.

Gorgeous. Sexy. Talented.

"Who is she?" Marissa asked, sitting across the couch and staring at him.

"Who is who?"

Marissa laughed wryly. "The woman you're thinking about right now, because it's certainly not me."

Xavier started to deny it, but she cut him off.

"C'mon, I'm in this dress." She motioned downward to the hot pink number. "Most men would be trying to take me home and get it off, but not you. You're looking off into the distance as if you can't wait to get out of here."

Xavier chuckled. "Really?"

"Oh, yes, baby," she purred. "You've got it bad."

"Nah, we're just kicking it," Xavier replied. And apparently Porscha had gotten bored with him, because she was looking to replace him.

"If you say so, but I think you have unfinished business. So let me give you a piece of advice. Talk to her."

Xavier wasn't sure if he should or even if he wanted to. He was angry with Porscha for going behind his back and dating another man. Although they hadn't defined the rules of their arrangement other than the secrecy she demanded, at the very least, he thought they were honest with one another.

"Thanks for the advice," Xavier said. "Can I give you a ride home?"

Marissa glanced around and noticed her two girl-friends had gone, most likely home with Allen or one of his friends, and it was just the two of them. "Yes, I would like that. Otherwise, I'd have to call an Uber."

"No worries," Xavier said. "I've got you covered."

The crowd was winding down, so they easily made it outside with minimal disruption. Xavier's driver was waiting outside. He opened the car door and Xavier and Marissa slid inside the limo.

Nobody noticed the photographer across the street snapping pictures.

Ten

*Xavier Lockett leaving men's club with unidentified
female. Who is the mystery woman?*

Porscha scanned the online post Erin showed her
early the next morning as they sat in her bedroom going
over next week's agenda. She tried to temper her response and not show how upset she was. "Thanks for
showing me this, Erin."

"I wasn't sure if I should," her assistant replied. "But
I knew you would want to know."

Was this his retaliation to her date with Ryan?

Xavier had ignored her texts and calls all week. And
now this? He was clearly telling her he didn't give a
damn who she was with because he was having fun
himself. But could she blame him? She'd set all of this
in motion but her date with the famous actor was just a

media ploy. Xavier going home from a nightclub with a beautiful woman was a direct hit to her solar plexus. If he wanted to strike back at her, he'd achieved his goal.

She was angry.

She was jealous.

Porscha wanted to tell him where he could go. That she didn't want or need him. But for now, she'd bide her time.

She had a workout with her trainer lined up and then the rest of the day was free before she had to be back on set tomorrow afternoon. Filming was winding down and Porscha couldn't be happier.

The last week had been wild. The media furor over her date with Ryan hadn't died down. In fact, it had only grown stronger as the week progressed. There were rumors she and Ryan were lovers, that they were getting married. It was all hogwash, but both their teams played coy with the press, releasing statements that they'd enjoyed the evening. When asked about future dates, Porscha told her mom to evade the question.

Ryan was a nice person, but he wasn't Xavier. She wanted to tell Xavier she'd made a mistake, but he'd ignored her attempts to rectify the situation. Instead, he'd gone out, found a hot chick and bedded her.

"You ready for your workout?" her trainer asked, coming into the room and clapping her hands. "We have to keep you fit for your tour coming up this summer."

"I'm ready." Porscha rose to her feet. She would use her frustration about Xavier's silence to fuel her workout.

And it worked.

Until the hour was over.

But then her anger at the situation came roaring back and her mind wouldn't settle. Glancing at her watch, she saw it was still only 9:00 a.m. If she hurried and had the private jet fueled, they could take off in a couple of hours. She would make it to Atlanta by evening and she and Xavier could have it out.

It was the only way she would get peace of mind. She refused to mope on her day off. She knew it was crazy to fly across the country when she had to be on the set tomorrow afternoon, but it was time she and Xavier cleared the air about where their relationship stood.

Xavier slept in on Sunday because he was recovering from a major hangover. He wasn't used to staying out late anymore, hanging with the fellas and drinking. Those days were long behind him. He stayed home all day, relaxing and watching television. He had no plans and was looking at a solitary evening. His siblings were all coupled up and his parents were going out to dinner with another family.

Xavier was left alone with his thoughts and his phone. Call him a masochist, but he scoured the internet and social media looking for more images of Porscha and Ryan. He knew it was stupid, but he couldn't stop himself. From what he could tell, the gossip sites were still rehashing Porscha's date with Ryan.

And why did it bother him so much who she was dating anyway? Women should be allowed to date more than one man. He'd certainly dated more than one woman. Women came to him at the snap of his fingers, and over time he'd become jaded by too much choice and opportunity. He'd enjoyed sex with them like any other red-blooded male, but it equaled lust and satisfaction, nothing more.

He'd become good at cordoning off his feelings, but Porscha was different. She could have any man she wanted, but she wanted him. Perhaps that was the turn-on. Now that she'd signaled that she didn't need him, it made him want her more. And though he wasn't looking to get married or have children, Xavier did want exclusivity. He wanted to be the *only* man Porscha was sleeping with. And the fact she didn't see it the same way had his pulse racing.

He was about to get off the couch and scrounge up some dinner when he heard gravel crunch in the driveway. He wasn't expecting anyone and went over to peer out the window. A stretch limousine had just pulled up to his door.

Who in the hell?

Xavier didn't have to wait long to find out who his mystery visitor was, because the driver came around to open the passenger door. To his shock, Porscha emerged, wearing an edgy black leather jacket over a utilitarian yet chic white jumpsuit and carrying a Louis Vuitton duffel bag. Xavier pushed the curtains back. He hadn't expected her visit, but he was glad she'd come. There was a lot that needed to be said and there was no time like the present.

Xavier didn't wait for her to knock. Instead he went to the door and opened it wide. Porscha stepped into the entry, and they stared at each other for several long moments. Xavier broke first.

"I'm surprised you could find the time to visit with

your busy dating life. Did you come to slum it?" he inquired. "Or are you here for a quickie before you have to get back to Ryan Mills?"

He knew the words were cruel, so he wasn't surprised when Porscha came toward him and pushed him back, with her palms on his chest. He stumbled inside the house and she followed behind him, slamming the door.

"You don't get to do that." She pointed her finger at him. "You don't get to be mad at me, Xavier. Not after the stunt you pulled last night." She took out her phone and brought up an image of him and the beautiful woman he'd left the nightclub with.

"Like hell I don't," he said, righting himself to face her. Although he had no idea who took the photo, he had nothing to be ashamed of. "You're the one who started us down this path, Porscha. So you sure as hell don't get to come to *my* home and tell me what to think or how to feel."

"And how do you feel, Xavier?" Porscha asked, removing her leather jacket and flinging it over the back of his sofa. "Please tell me, because you didn't answer any of my calls or texts."

"Why would I? You were with another man!"

"Damn it, Xavier. Answer me! I just flew thousands of miles to come here tonight. The least I deserve is the truth."

"The truth?" Xavier asked, nearly shouting at her. "I don't think you know it, Porscha, because if you did, you would have told me about your date with Ryan much sooner, but you didn't."

"Did I have to? Since when? I don't owe you anything. And you didn't seem to care last night when you were all over another woman."

"I'm only following your lead."

"I didn't sleep with Ryan!" she yelled at him. "The only reason I went out with him was for publicity."

"And I didn't sleep with the woman last night, either," he responded hotly. "I needed to blow off some steam with my friends, but therein lies the problem. You may not *owe* me anything, Porscha, but you don't share anything with me, either. You could have told me about the media stunt, but you didn't. You set all the rules and I'm supposed to go along with them like a good little puppy dog? Well, guess what? That doesn't work for me."

"I'm sorry. I should have told you."

"Finally, we're getting somewhere, so let me be clear on another topic. I don't want you to date other men."

"Why not?" She continued pressing him.

"Because I'm jealous!" Xavier roared. "It kills me to see you with another man. Knowing he's touching you, possibly kissing you. Those lips—" he looked at her pink-tinted lips "—belong to me."

A slow smile spread across her face at his words, and he could see her pulse point beating frantically at the base of her throat. He had the inexplicable urge to cover it with his lips. With his tongue. "My lips are my own."

"You think so?" Xavier said, storming toward her. They stared at each other; both were breathing hard with the exertion of keeping their distance. "Would you like me to prove you belong to me?"

Her pupils dilated and her eyes darkened with desire. "Yes, if you dare."

Xavier hauled Porscha toward him and nudged her thighs wider with his knee so she could feel what she did to him. Her eyes flew to his. Then he lowered his head and touched his lips to hers in a searing kiss that told Porscha she was his in every way. She let him take control, so his tongue speared boldly into her mouth. She softened against him, allowing him to taste her essence, and her hands flattened over the hard muscles of his chest to slide upward and snake around his neck. Then she began moving her lips beneath his in an age-old request for more. Xavier gave it to her.

Nothing else mattered in that moment. Not his anger. Not Ryan Mills. It was just the two of them. And they came together like magic. Like it always was between them. When he lifted his head a fraction and they broke apart for air, he peered into her eyes. "Now, tell me again, you're not mine?"

How was it possible to feel so much for one person? To want so much.

Porscha knew it was emotional suicide to let her heart rule her actions, but her entire body had caught fire with Xavier's kiss. She wanted him even though she'd been furious when she arrived. She wanted everything Xavier could give her. Wasn't that why she'd come? Flown halfway across the country—*for this*?

She gripped the back of his head and tugged him back down. His mouth captured hers in a sweet, lingering kiss that caused her to moan for the aching pleasure only he could give her.

"Xavier."

He swept her into his arms and strode toward the

bedroom. "I'm going to make to love you, Porscha, and remind you how good it is between us. Until you won't so much as think about another man." His voice was raw and hoarse with need and Porscha believed him.

He lowered her to the bed, but Porscha rushed to get up on her knees, hastily pushing the hem of his T-shirt over his head and tossing it away while Xavier unzipped her jumpsuit. He clawed at the sleeves until he could slide them down her arms, then she was leaning back against the duvet so he could drag the entire garment along with her thong down her legs. Then he was un-buckling his pants and they followed the same path as his shirt. When he was naked as she, he smoothed on a condom and joined her on the bed.

"You drive me crazy," Xavier said, and then he was cupping her.

Porscha nearly dissolved when he parted her slick flesh and delved between her legs to glide his thumb and fingers over her in all the right places.

"Xavier, please—" she moaned.

He lowered his body on top of hers and his smooth thick hardness opened her up, penetrating deep in-side. For a minute, they were both completely still as if suspended between two worlds. Xavier's eyes looked dazed as they met hers. There was nowhere for her to hide. His eyes glittered with hunger and Porscha knew that when he took her this time, it wouldn't be slow and gentle. It was going to be fierce and urgent because he was going to claim her and make her his.

He did just that.

Xavier crashed his mouth down onto hers and his tongue thrust deep as he plunged deep inside her. He was up on his forearms, his body sliding over hers, each stroke more intimate than the next, winding her tighter and tighter. And when he opened his mouth wide to bear down on one of her nipples, she nearly screamed at the sensation of having his greedy mouth on her once again.

Porscha wrapped her legs around his hips, a torrent of need flooding her. Xavier drove into her harder and deeper and she simply clung on as he took her to new heights. He grunted in pleasure. "Tell me if I'm too rough."

She shook her head. "No. Give me more. I want more."

"Ah, hell, Porscha." He began moving faster. He was tipping her toward the edge of an exquisite release, the kind she had only ever experienced in his arms, making her his with each thrust. She almost didn't want to let go, but then she opened her eyes at that exact moment and found Xavier watching her. The connection was so elemental it hurtled them both over the cliff into a mind-blowing orgasm that had Xavier roaring out his pleasure and Porscha screaming.

Afterward, Xavier bent down and kissed her sweetly on the mouth. His big body swamped and cocooned her in a delicious warmth that made Porscha in her weakened state blissfully happy.

He'd proved his point.

She, or at least her body, belonged to him.

Eleven

Xavier wanted to feel relieved. He'd shown Porscha how good they were together. But he wasn't sure he could trust her. She hadn't been honest with him about the media stunt. Yes, she'd come to him tonight. For what? They hadn't yet settled anything between them or agreed to be exclusive. Instead, they'd done what they always did and torn each other's clothes off.

Porscha provoked a physical response in him he couldn't seem to understand. She simply took his breath away and he found himself consumed with her. He tried to analyze her appeal and what it was that kept him coming back for more. She was beautiful. Yes, she had a great body, and whenever they were together, desire, hot and hard, flared inside him, obliterating everything else in its path.

He felt murderous seeing her with Ryan. It was why he'd gone out with his boys and flirted with that woman, all in the hope he could beat whatever this was out of him. But he couldn't. Porscha was the sexiest woman he'd ever met. He didn't know why; he just knew it felt good and he wanted the feeling to last.

And so he made love to her again. This time it was different than the first. It was slow. He put his mouth on every inch of her body where he could find purchase, licking her one inch at a time. And when he settled between her legs, he drank deep of her core until she was sobbing out his name like an incantation.

Then he set her on her knees and with his hands on her hips, he took her from behind in a slow, steady rhythm that was so intense…it was too much…but not quite enough. Her cries of abandon filled the room, especially when he reached around her to push two fingers inside her. His thumb traced, found and circled the swollen bud and she gasped aloud, but he wasn't letting her go. His arm was clamped around her waist so he could pleasure her while simultaneously pressing farther inside her.

And when she was nearly pleading with him to end it and give her release, he flipped them so she was astride him and could take him deeper. He looked up at her and her head was thrown back as she rocked her hips wickedly against him.

"Look at me," he ordered.

Her eyes fluttered open, and she didn't look away as he began thrusting upward to meet her. She was right there with him and when the tempo began building, his thrusts became swift, sending excitement racing up his back. Porscha leaned forward, her breasts coming into direct contact with his face. He reached upward and laved one nipple lightly with his tongue. That was all it took for her to fly apart. Her detonation was something otherworldly and caused a deeply animalistic growl to escape his lips as Xavier met her in a state of utter ecstasy.

Porscha awakened in the middle of the night slightly disoriented. She felt different. Her entire world had been upended. Somehow Xavier had managed to strip away all her bravado as well as her willpower and made her a mass of sexual need. If he was in her presence, she wanted him to touch her. If he touched her, she wanted him to make love to her. Her desire for him was all-consuming, so much so she'd flown here to Atlanta when she was due back at Los Angeles to be on the set by early afternoon tomorrow.

But they did need to talk. She couldn't, wouldn't leave until they did. Until she understood what he wanted, what they both wanted to make sure this arrangement worked for both of them. Because she'd heard resentment in Xavier's tone when he mentioned doing things her way. And she'd insisted on conducting the affair on her terms to protect herself from him. She'd never once considered how he might feel.

She was going to do that now.

"Xavier." She shook his shoulder.

"Hmm…," he said sleepily.

"We need to talk."

He turned around, glanced at the clock and tried

to pull her back down onto the pillows. "We can talk tomorrow."

"No." Porscha reached for the lamp sitting on the nightstand and turned it on, flooding the room with light. "It has to be now."

Xavier sighed and rubbed the sleep from his eyes as he sat upright. As much as she loved his muscled chest and firm abs, she needed to stay focused. She couldn't leave until they had a discussion like two normal adults. She would go first.

"I'm sorry," she said. "I'm sorry I didn't tell you about Ryan sooner. I should have, but honestly, I was afraid. Afraid of how you might react if I mentioned dating another man."

"Damn right! I don't like it."

"Fair enough. I only agreed to the date with Ryan because my mother suggested it would be good for my career and boost sales for the album."

"And that's your excuse?"

She lowered her head in embarrassment. "Yes. And it's the truth."

"Porscha, I've known you to go against your mother if you felt strongly enough. You didn't in this instance. It tells me a lot." He threw back the covers and started toward the bathroom.

"Xavier...wait!" Porscha followed him, uncaring of her nakedness. "Why are you mad? You proved your point when you went out with your friends and flirted with that beautiful woman."

She watched as he turned on the taps to the shower. "I'm not mad. You've told me the truth, so now I know."

Her brows furrowed. "So why do I feel as if nothing has changed between us?"

"What's changed is that I want exclusivity, Porscha," Xavier said. "I didn't think I had to spell it out since we're sleeping together, but I'm saying it again." He stepped into the shower and Porscha didn't hesitate to join him.

"I want that, too." She smiled, circling her arms around his naked waist and looking up at him. She didn't care if she got her hair wet. "You're the only man I want to be with." She stroked his cheek with her palm. "In fact, I haven't been with another man since we've been together all these months."

He raised a brow.

"It's true. I know you may find that hard to believe, but it is. And as far as the date is concerned, nothing happened with me and him other than a boring dinner and a choreographed outing to a nightclub."

"Will you see him again?" Xavier asked.

"Probably not."

Xavier pushed her away. "If you don't mind, I think I can shower alone."

"Don't push me away, Xavier," Porscha said, moving toward him again. "I don't want Ryan. I want you." She went to take his hardness in her hands, but he gripped her arms to stop her, even as he hauled her toward him.

"We can't. I need a condom."

"Where?"

"Bottom drawer in the cabinet by the sink."

Porscha stepped out of the shower long enough to grab a foil packet, and when she returned, they picked up where they left off. They reached for each other at the same time, kissing and touching. The passion between them was a strong as ever despite the fact there were still unresolved issues between them.

But it all went away the moment their bodies connected. Porscha felt an emotional bond to Xavier as deep as the physical one they shared. Their foreheads touched and they began moving together as one. She could hold nothing back and soon her world splintered into a trillion pieces.

Xavier swore as he continued driving into her. With her back against the shower wall, Porscha wound her legs around his waist as yet another orgasm began to roll through her. Unable to contain his own climax, Xavier threw back his head and shouted out his release. In that moment, Porscha realized it wasn't just about phenomenal sex anymore. She was developing feelings for Xavier. Feelings she wondered if she'd had all along, ever since they first met.

"Do you have to go?" Xavier asked when instead of coming back to his bed after their shower interlude, she dressed. His clock read 7:00 a.m.

"Thank God, you're a couple of hours ahead, but yes. I must get back. We're wrapping up filming soon," she replied.

He nodded. "Okay, let me get dressed. I'll walk you out."

She shook her head. "No, let me remember you like this." She glanced at his bare chest and continued moving her hands lower until she could open the towel around his waist. "All sexy and very—" she paused for a beat when she laid eyes on his length "—very aroused."

"You sure you don't want to help me take care of that," he said with an unabashed grin.

"Afraid not. I have to get a move on it, if I want to make it back to the West Coast." She was silent for several moments and then asked, "Are we good?"

"Sure." But even as he said the word, Xavier wasn't sure. She had never definitively answered his question about whether she would stop seeing Ryan for publicity. Instead, she'd sexed him up in the shower until he could no longer remember his own name.

Porscha sighed. "I'm not convinced. Listen, Xavier. I promise I will keep you in the loop going forward."

"And Ryan?"

"The media attention will fade once I make it clear it was a one-time thing. You'll see." She glanced down at her watch. "I have to go." She brushed her soft lips over his, but he didn't let her leave so fast. His hands tangled in her hair and he brought her mouth toward his in a demanding kiss. She groaned with pleasure, but gently removed herself from his embrace.

"You don't play fair. I'll call you from the plane." And with that, she left the house.

Xavier heard the click of the front door as she closed it. He folded his arms behind his head and thought about last night. Porscha's visit had been a surprise. After seeing her with Ryan, he'd assumed their affair was over. He'd anticipated receiving the brush-off. Instead, Porscha had come to him and admitted she'd made a mistake. She'd agreed to his request for exclusivity and claimed he was the only man she'd been with. He wanted to believe her, but he wasn't sure.

He remembered Tyra Daniels, a woman he'd casually dated, and the lie she'd told. She'd claimed he was the father of her baby, which could have destroyed his career. Luckily, the truth had come out because his father had put Nico Shapiro, the Lockett organization's investigator, on the case. Nico's sleuthing had revealed that Tyra had been sleeping with several members of the team, not just him. She'd known Xavier wasn't the father based on the timeline of when the child was conceived, but she lied deliberately because she wanted the fame and money that came with the Lockett name. Xavier could have been caught up in quite the scandal. He supposed it was why he had such a hard time trusting women and believing Porscha when she said it was over with her and Ryan.

He hoped that she was being truthful, but was he fooling himself because he didn't want to give her up?

Twelve

Porscha arrived back in Los Angeles just in the nick of time. It was just past 10:00 a.m. on the West Coast, and she had just enough time to get home and changed to be on set by noon. She'd only had a few hours of sleep on the plane, but she wouldn't have traded her night jaunt to Atlanta for anything. She'd been angry, jealous and confused when she'd flown there, with no idea how she would be received.

Xavier had been angry because she hadn't told him about her date with Ryan beforehand. But he'd also admitted he hadn't deliberately set out to hurt her by being photographed with another woman. He'd gone out with his boys to get her out of his system, but he couldn't. She couldn't let him go, either; he had entered her bloodstream like a powerful drug.

As she took in the scenic view on the way to the Pacific Palisades, all Porscha thought about was Xavier. About the way he made her gasp out his name orgasm after orgasm. How he stroked her skin and whispered to her about how her body was everything a woman's body should be. Her senses were reeling, and she could still taste him on her lips.

God, she was in serious trouble of falling for him as she had in Denver. Was she a fool for believing in the same man twice? Xavier had the power to break her heart all over again and Porscha was scared senseless. Her mind told her to retreat. Take this time away from him to be sure Xavier was what she really wanted, but her body…her body craved his and she wondered how she would ever live without his kind of pleasure.

The limo slowed and soon they were easing into the driveway of her home. Her mother was standing outside the doorway dressed in jeans and a light sweater, but the look on her face wasn't casual. It was angry.

Porscha sucked in a breath. After her magical night with Xavier, she was in no mood for her mother's histrionics. She was no errant schoolgirl coming home after a night out.

When Jose came and opened her door, Porscha slid out. "Hello." She greeted her mother with a kiss on the cheek and was about to walk inside the foyer, but Diane was on her heels.

"Well? Are you not going to talk about the elephant in the room?"

Porscha spun around. "Which is what exactly, Mom?"

"That you left Los Angeles without a word to me," her mother replied swiftly.

"I didn't realize I had to answer to you about my whereabouts every single second of every single day. I'm a grown woman." She turned and began stalking up the staircase. She needed to shower and head to the set, but her mother wasn't letting this go. Diane followed her to her bedroom.

"For Christ's sake, Mom. Back off!" Porscha yelled.

"I won't! Not when I see you making a horrible mistake."

"According to you," Porscha said and started stripping off her leather jacket. "The great all-seeing Diane Childs who knows everything and thinks she knows best. You don't."

When she was down to her undies, Porscha walked to her master bath and to the sink to brush her teeth. Yet again, her mother was in the doorway.

"He's going to hurt you, Porscha. *Again.*"

Porscha slammed down her toothbrush and faced her. "You don't know that."

"I know how devastated you were when you got back from the clinic. You were there to heal from losing your father and your career tanking and you came back with another heartbreak."

"I misunderstood the situation," Porscha replied. "Plus, this isn't the same thing. *I hurt him* this time. *I* went on a date with Ryan."

"And what did he do? Did he call you up to find out what happened?" her mother asked. "No, he went right into the arms of another woman. Erin showed me the post."

"What did you do, Mom, browbeat my assistant until

she gave up my location?" Only Erin had known she was with Xavier.

Her mother lowered her head and didn't answer. Instead, she said, "I only want what's best for you. Why is that so hard to believe?"

"I don't have time for this. I have to shower. Can I get some privacy?"

Her mother stared at her for what seemed like an eternity before she pushed off the doorway and slammed the door shut behind her. Porscha was thankful to be alone. She wanted her mother to be wrong in her prediction that she and Xavier would end up like they had nearly four years ago. This time *could* and *would* be different.

"You have three and a half minutes left," the producer told Xavier in his ear as he finished wrapping up his *Q and A on Atlanta Sports Night* segment later that morning.

Xavier continued asking the questions on the script on the screen in front of him, but if he had his way, he would be on a football field instead of just talking to a player. He ended the interview shortly afterward and allowed one of the production crew to take off his mic.

"Thanks, Dan." He was walking off the set but stopped when he saw a familiar face standing off to the side. She was dressed in a red suit dress and four-inch heels and looked every bit the CEO that she was.

"Giana, what you are you doing here?" Xavier asked, pulling her into his arms for a hug and a kiss.

"I was hoping I could take my little brother to

lunch," Giana replied once they parted. "If you didn't have any plans."

"None at all."

"Excellent." She looped her arm in his and together they walked toward the bank of elevators down the hall. "So, what's new with you? I feel like you've been quiet of late."

"I've been busy."

"With a certain female?" Giana asked.

"Are you fishing for details, big sis?" Xavier asked, peering down at her.

"Absolutely. And you can tell me over lunch."

Once outside, they walked a short distance to a nearby restaurant the ASN staff liked to frequent. The food was good and the service top-notch. The ambience was grand with dark oak paneling and white tablecloths. After they were seated and the waiter had taken their orders, an ahi tuna bowl for Giana and a salmon salad for him, his sister wasted no time going in for the details.

"What's this I hear about Porscha Childs dating Ryan Mills?" Giana asked, filling her glass from a bottle of Perrier on the table.

"The date was purely for show."

"That's not what I heard. There's rumors they've been seeing each other the entire time they've been filming."

"All of which are unsubstantiated and false," Xavier responded. "C'mon, Giana. Do I look like the type of man that likes to share?"

Giana shrugged. "Hey, you're my baby brother. I

have no idea what you like to do in the bedroom, and I don't want to know."

Xavier laughed heartily. "You, my dear, have an overactive imagination like everyone else in America. Just because the press says it's true doesn't make it so. You recall that's how rumors got started about me fathering Tyra's baby when I was in college."

A serious expression returned to Giana's face. "Yes, I do. How could I forget? Daddy was furious about how the negative press might sideline your career. And he wasn't having it."

"It's one of the few times I appreciated his heavy-handedness. If he hadn't hired Nico, Tyra would have ruined me."

"Fortunately, that didn't happen, and you still went on to win the Heisman," Giana responded.

Xavier nodded and his mind drifted to accepting the award onstage. How happy he'd been and how everything had seemed possible back then. He came back to earth when he felt his sister's hands covering his and giving them a gentle squeeze.

"I'm sorry. I shouldn't have brought it up."

He shook his head. "You can't walk on eggshells around me forever, Gigi. I've learned to deal with the hand I've been dealt, but on occasion, the memories pop up. I'm starting to think of them more fondly now."

"That's good to hear," Giana replied with a half smile.

Their lunch entrées arrived shortly afterward, and they tucked into their meals with gusto. That was when Giana returned to the original topic of conversation. "I'm curious, Xavier. If the date with Ryan Mills was just for the media, what does that mean for you and Porscha?"

"We're not looking to get serious, if that's what you're after."

"No?" Giana quirked a brow. "Wynn told me you were quite upset at the gym when you heard about it."

"I was jealous, but Porscha explained the situation."

"When?"

Xavier smiled as he thought about Porscha astride him during the wee hours of the morning, taking him to heaven. "Last night. She flew in to see me."

"And you didn't take the day off to be with her today?" Giana inquired. "Xavier..." She shook her head in dismay.

He laughed. "I'm not completely dense, Gigi. Porscha left this morning. She had to get back to the film set. I'm sure I'll see her again."

"You're telling me she literally flew overnight to be with you?" Giana inquired. "Hmm..."

"What does that 'hmm' mean?"

"It means that you claim the two of you aren't a couple or getting serious, but you were quick to anger when you thought she was with another man. And a woman doesn't just fly cross-country overnight and back again for someone she doesn't care about."

"You're wrong. Porscha has always been clear about what she wants from me. And now, that's dating and sex *exclusively*."

Giana brows furrowed. "If you say so. Listen, will I see you at Julian and Elyse's baby shower on Saturday?"

"I guess. I was invited."

"You'll have fun. Just wait and see."

But her words gave Xavier pause. Was there more to his and Porscha's relationship than he was willing to admit? He had come to care for her, and she wasn't just a bedmate anymore, if she'd ever been. In the past, he had never wanted love in his life. There hadn't been any room for it because he had to keep his mind clear and sharp for football. But it wasn't clear or sharp right now. Whenever he and Porscha were apart, it left an ache.

This morning when they'd been in the shower with their foreheads against each other and their bodies fused together as if they were designed to fit, like two pieces cut from the same mold, Xavier had wondered if there was more yet to be discovered between them. And if so, was he finally ready to make room in his life and his heart for love?

Thirteen

"The press isn't happy that we aren't fueling the fire," Ryan said after he and Porscha finished filming later that day and he walked her back to her trailer. "I think everyone was expecting the next Brad and Angelina."

Porscha chuckled. "I'm sorry to disappoint them, but…" She was trying to figure out a way to say she wasn't interested, without hurting Ryan's feelings. He was a big star, and she knew he'd lobbied for her to get the role after she screen-tested with him, but she couldn't ignore her feelings after last night.

She and Xavier had agreed to be exclusive.

And after what happened in Denver, it was a big deal. The trust issue between them wasn't completely resolved. She'd sensed that in Xavier's response to her this morning in the shower and when she'd left. If she went back on her word and continued to date Ryan, it would make any sort of relationship between them untenable.

"But...?" Ryan prompted her to continue.

"There's someone else," Porscha answered honestly.

"And they don't understand what this means?" Ryan asked, cocking his head to one side and peering at her. "It's just publicity to help our careers. They should understand. You can still see them in private."

"Why should we have to?" Porsha whispered. "It was all a media stunt anyway."

"Sounds like he means something to you."

Porscha nodded because Ryan was right.

She had developed feelings for Xavier, but it was so complicated because it was mixed in with past hurt. It wasn't easy letting go and making herself vulnerable again.

"All right, I won't push," Ryan responded. "But I do think it's a wasted opportunity." He left her alone in the trailer, but not for long. Her mother was climbing the stairs to be with her shortly afterward.

"I just spoke to Ryan. He told me you're done with dating him."

"That's right."

"I think it's a mistake, Porscha."

"Well, I didn't ask for your opinion," Porscha replied sharply. "This is my life. *I* get to decide."

Her mother frowned at her. "You really think you're in love with a former quarterback with a bum knee you met while you were in a mental health clinic? You were out of your mind with grief, and he wasn't in his right state, either."

Porscha's eyes grew wide. She couldn't believe her mother could be so cruel and unfeeling. Or that she thought so little of Porscha's judgment. "Out!" She pointed to the door.

"Porscha, I'm sorry." Diane started toward her, but Porscha backed away.

"I said I want you out now!"

Diane held up her hands. "All right, I'll leave, but I'll be close by." She started down the stairs and stopped. "I'll be right outside if you need me." She glanced at Erin, who was behind her on the trailer steps. "Take care of her."

"Ohmigod!" Porscha scrubbed her hands across her face and plopped down onto the small sofa couch.

"Are you okay?" Erin asked, coming to sit beside her. "Should I leave you alone, too?"

"No, no." Porscha shook her head as tears slid down her cheeks. "You've been wonderful, Erin. Thank you so much. What would I ever do without you? I'm so sorry my mother harassed you while I was in Atlanta. She had no right to. You work for me."

"It's okay."

"No, it's not," Porscha replied. "She crossed the line."

"Don't worry about it. I'm okay. It's nothing I'm not used to," Erin responded.

Erin had been a godsend and a wonderful edition to her team the last few years. She was smart and savvy and Porscha knew she wouldn't be able to hold on to her long, but she was happy to have a confidante. Someone she could trust.

Right now, that person wasn't her mother. She knew

Diane could be cold and heartless, but usually it was never directed at Porscha. She'd always thought it was for other people, never her, but the line between mother and manager had been blurred for far too long.

Porscha was going to have to make some changes.

"I can't believe men are required to come to baby showers now," Xavier said as he, Julian, Roman, Wynn and Silas stood outside on the terrace of the Lockett mansion in Tuxedo Park while the women in their family oohed and aahed over baby clothes, bassinets and the like.

The rest of the week had gone fast. Although he and Porscha were apart, they texted and spoke on the phone as often as her schedule permitted. And certainly, more than they'd done in the past. It seemed that by his telling Porscha he wanted exclusivity, somehow they'd walked themselves into a relationship. And Xavier didn't mind so long as she didn't hear wedding bells.

"I don't know when it happened, either," Roman said with a chuckle, "but men are no longer on the sidelines handing out cigars in the waiting room when the baby is born. Oh, no, we are in the thick of it, from the birthing classes to the delivery, to taking off for paternity leave to help with the baby."

"We haven't told anyone, but Janelle and I are expecting as well, so I'll be looking to you guys for advice when the time comes," Silas said from the sidelines.

"Congratulations." Wynn stepped in and gave his best friend a one-armed hug while everyone else shook his hand. "I'm happy for you. I know you both have wanted a family for a long time."

"We have. Janelle is excited and we've been reading *What To Expect When You're Expecting*."

"Pregnancy has been eye-opening," Julian said, taking a swig of his beer. "We started Lamaze classes about a month ago."

"Lord! Am I honestly standing here talking about birthing classes with my brothers?" Xavier asked in a huff.

"Hey, don't knock it, Xavier," Roman said, laughing. "The same thing could happen to you one day."

Xavier shook his head. "Me? A father. I don't think so." He honestly never thought about being a parent. It wasn't like he believed he would be a bad one, but it had never crossed his mind. It always seemed like far-off in the future. Maybe because he'd never met someone he wanted to marry.

But if anyone could make him *want* to consider marriage, it would be Porscha.

Julian snorted. "I think I said that, too. And look at me now. Mr. Playboy himself about to be a father, but I have to tell you, X—" he glanced at the doorway to the house "—I'm the happiest I've ever been. Elyse completes me in every way."

"Oh, now you're sounding like a sap." Roman laughed.

"Make fun all you want," Julian returned, pointing a finger at him. "You were head over heels for *my friend* and I recall how extremely territorial you were when it came to Shantel."

"Don't you start with that 'my friend' stuff," Roman growled.

"See?" Julian turned to Xavier, laughing.

"He's right, Roman," Xavier responded. "You are acting possessive. Admit it."

"That I adore my wife?" Roman asked. "Absolutely." He turned to Julian. "You not showing up at that bachelor auction was the best thing that ever happened to me."

Julian was supposed to attend the auction with Shantel but had been a no-show, leaving Shantel alone to bid on Roman instead. One thing had led to another and soon Shantel was not only wearing Roman's ring, but carrying his baby.

"See? I'm indirectly responsible for the two of you getting together," Julian shrugged. "You should be thanking me."

"Julian!" Elyse's voice rang out from inside the manor.

"You're being summoned," Roman teased.

Julian rolled his eyes at their older brother before heading inside.

"I'm glad you both are happy," Xavier said, "but don't wish your domesticity upon me."

"Maybe not domesticity, but certainly love and affection," Roman replied. "With someone who is worthy of you."

Xavier rolled his eyes upward. "Not you, too. Don't judge Porscha harshly. I already told Giana that Porscha dating Ryan was a media stunt. Get to know her before you say she isn't good enough for me."

"Oh, I know," Roman responded. "Giana told me. I just worry about you, Xavier. You've always been rather guarded when it came to the opposite sex, especially after that incident with Tyra."

"Wouldn't you? She tried to ruin my reputation," Xavier pointed out. "It's why I talked to Curtis and Wayne and told them my cautionary tale. I wouldn't want them or any of our players in a similar circumstance. It's extremely easy to get caught up these days."

"You're being careful. And I get that," Roman said, "but Porscha means something to you, or you would have let her go months ago. And on that note, we're being called in."

"For what?"

"You'll see."

Several minutes later, Xavier found himself along with Roman, Julian, Wynn and Silas in a baby-bottle chugging contest to see which of them could finish sucking all the apple juice out of the tiny hole in the bottle first. Xavier won that round, but the games continued with a good, old-fashioned change-the-diaper-blindfolded game. Roman took that win thanks to lots of practice changing Ethan while being half asleep.

Then there was the great stroller race. Everyone went onto the terrace to watch the men race across an obstacle course in the backyard without crashing their strollers with baby dolls inside. Julian was much faster on his feet and won the race hands down.

Afterward, they retired back to the main living room where their mother, Angelique, had laid out an amazing spread for the guests. After Elyse and Julian made their plates and the ladies dug in, Xavier filled his plate with veggies from the crudités platter, along with quiche, tea sandwiches, Swedish meatballs, chicken satay, mini mac-and-cheese bites and bacon-wrapped scallops.

"This is delicious, Mom," Elyse said from the sofa.

"You really outdid yourself." Xavier's sister-in-law had taken to calling their mother Mom because her own mother had died from cancer when she was young.

"You're absolutely welcome, my darling," his mother said from the chair opposite her. She was looking like a refined hostess in a yellow one-shoulder batwing cape dress that reached her knees. "Has everyone had enough to eat?" She glanced at Xavier's full plate, then up at him, and winked.

Xavier went to the dining room to escape from the couples and babies some of Elyse's friends had brought with them. He was settling down to his meal when his father walked in and sat across from him.

"I see I'm not the only one escaping all the brou-haha."

"Yeah, there are too many women and babies in there," Xavier said. "Don't want it to rub off."

His father eyed him. "Of all my sons, I thought you'd embrace fatherhood."

"Why is that?"

"Because you probably had more of my time and attention than even Roman."

That wasn't always a good thing, Xavier thought, but he continued eating and chose not to comment. His father wanted something. He was a calculating man and wouldn't have followed Xavier in here otherwise.

"I'm really proud of everything you've done with the foundation, and I hear the mentorship with the players is going well."

"And?"

"I'm wondering if you're finally ready to come back to the fold?" Josiah asked.

And there it was. The real reason his father came to talk to him.

"Coaching."

His father nodded. "Being a sportscaster isn't your thing and you and I both know it. It was only a stop-gap measure to keep your head in the game and not fall into a deep depression after you couldn't play football anymore."

"And you think you know me so well?"

"I know the son I raised sacrificed everything for the love of the game."

"Those days are over."

"Playing, yes, but you are talented, Xavier. You always have been. I saw it in you when you were just a young boy. It's still there, if you can only believe in yourself like I do."

"You don't think I'm a failure?" Xavier asked.

"Have I ever said that?"

"No, but it was implied in the disappointment in your eyes."

"Yes, I was disappointed *for* you, but not *in* you. Never in you," his father responded. "And I'm sorry you felt that way. I wish you had told me, because I would have corrected you. Told you how immensely proud I am to have you as my boy."

"How can you be?" Xavier wondered aloud. "I didn't live up to my full potential."

"Life handed you a raw deal," his father said. "And you wallowed in it for a couple of months. But when the going got tough, you dug your heels in and brought yourself back to the other side. Reinvented yourself. How could I not be proud?"

Xavier was about to say more, but then his cell phone rang.

The display read Porscha. "Excuse me for a minute, Dad." Xavier left the dining room to walk into the corridor and take the call.

"Xavier, it's me," Porscha said from the other end of the line.

"Why are you whispering?" he inquired.

"I'm outside."

"Outside where?"

"Your parents' gate," Porscha said. "I called but your butler refused to buzz me in so the security guard won't open the gate. He didn't believe me when I told him I was Porscha Childs. He said the family wasn't expecting any guests."

"You're here!" It was impossible. Xavier raced down the hall, grabbed a key fob for the gate from the entryway and was out the front door as if he was the quarterback he used to be. It was harder for him to run because of his injury, and he quickly found himself stopping abruptly halfway down the driveway.

He was close enough to the see the front gate, and sure enough, Porscha was standing there. He pushed the button on the fob and soon the gates were cranking open, and to his delight Porscha ran toward him, wearing a baseball cap, jeans and a bomber jacket.

He hugged her and she held on to him tightly as if she never wanted to let him go. When they finally parted, he could see something was horribly wrong. Her tawny-brown cheeks were stained with tears and her eyes were red and puffy.

"Dear God, Porscha." Xavier tilted her chin upward to face him. "What happened?"

"It's awful." Porscha leaned her head against his chest and began sobbing.

"It's okay," Xavier said, lifting her into his arms. "I've got you." He carried her away from the main house and toward the guesthouse. No one would bother them there.

When they arrived, Xavier walked over to the couch with Porscha still in his arms and sat down. He rubbed her back as she cried until eventually her tears subsided and she grew quiet. He had no idea what could have upset her and why she was in Atlanta alone without her bodyguard Jose or any support. He wasn't going to pry, though; she would tell him when she was ready. They were silent until she finally spoke.

"Filming stopped because the director asked for some scene rewrites, so I headed home. As soon as I left the set, I was accosted by the press. My assistant, Erin, the woman I've trusted with my entire life the last three years, sold me out," Porscha said.

"Really? Erin's always been so great and supportive. What did she do?" Xavier inquired.

"She told the press I was hospitalized for a mental breakdown. She told them about Denver."

"Oh, no! Sweetheart, I'm so sorry," Xavier said and clutched her to his chest a bit tighter. How had he not heard about this? Then it dawned on him: he'd turned off the notifications about Porscha on his phone after her date with Ryan and he'd never turned them back on.

"I can't believe I trusted her," Porscha sniffed. "Erin has been my go-to person since I got out of the clinic.

The person I relied on, other than my mother, and she *betrayed* me."

"That's horrible. I'm so sorry, babe." Xavier squeezed her tight against his chest.

"I've always treated her with nothing but respect. I paid her two times the normal salary because, silly me, I thought I was buying loyalty and trust, but at the first sign of a big payout, she stabbed me in the back."

"It's going to be all right."

"How?" she cried, glancing up at him. "How can it be? America thinks I'm disingenuous because I lied. I told everyone I was exhausted after my father died. No one knew I'd gone to the clinic for my mental health."

"You can't blame yourself for what happened. Erin betrayed your trust. That's not your fault."

"Yes, it is, Xavier. It makes me feel like I can't trust my own judgment. First Gil and now Erin." Her head fell back against his chest. "Am I fooling myself about you, too?"

He grabbed her chin and forced her to look at him. He didn't know who Gil was, but Porscha would tell him about it when she was ready. "If you thought that, you wouldn't be here, Porscha. You know you can trust me. I'm here for you, babe."

She nodded. "Thank you. I just need a place to lie low for a while and get my head on straight."

"Then you found it," Xavier said. "I will protect you."

Fourteen

Porscha awoke the next morning and at first, she didn't know where she was. All she could see was turquoise waters from a bedroom door that opened out to the ocean. The furniture in the room was white and lacquered, and a white shag rug lay on the floor. Across the hall, she caught a glimpse of a modern bathroom.

She most certainly wasn't in her Palisades home where a crowd of paparazzi were probably staked out in front. Then it came back to her. Erin's betrayal. Porscha had never wanted anyone to know about her mental breakdown. It was her truth, no one else's, and now the entire world knew her secret.

Looking around, she knew she wasn't in Xavier's guesthouse, either, where Xavier had taken her yesterday when she'd been in a state of sheer panic. She'd felt as if the walls were closing in on her and there was nowhere and no one to turn to.

Only one person had come to her mind in her distress.

Xavier.

She hadn't known why. She just wanted someone else to take the wheel because she clearly wasn't good at it. And right now, she felt as if Xavier had lived up to his promise.

She felt protected.

Cared for.

Loved?

No, she mustn't think the word because love was not part of the equation when it came to them. Yet in her darkest hour, the person she thought of first had been Xavier. It hadn't been her mother, who had wasted no time reminding Porscha she was a loser for having put her faith and trust in another human.

Porscha hadn't wanted to hear that. She just wanted to be comforted. Held. But Diane didn't know how to do that.

But Xavier did. After crying on his expensive shirt yesterday afternoon, he'd chartered his father's jet and flown them to Turks and Caicos last night.

Xavier made her feel as if she could take on the world as long as she had him by her side. Throwing back the covers, Porscha found herself not nude as she would have imagined after a night spent with Xavier, but rather wearing an Atlanta Cougars T-shirt. It had to be Xavier's, but it fit her like a dress.

She heard music playing from somewhere in the house and followed the sound, padding barefoot down the hall. She quickly noted the color palette in the home ranged from white to splashes of turquoise. The decor was beachy, with an island feel and rattan furniture. She found Xavier in the small kitchen, which was modern, with white cabinets and stainless steel appliances.

He was bare-chested, and she took in the line of hair that arrowed down his stomach past the waistband of the shorts he wore. Porscha's throat felt as dry as the desert and she couldn't breathe, let alone speak. Xavier was so brutally sexy. She longed to touch his chest and tease his nipples with her tongue. She sucked in a quick breath. She very much needed the physical connection they shared with each other.

He was at the kitchen island with three wicker stools tucked neatly underneath. He was dicing vegetables and singing the Wayne Wonder song, "No Letting Go."

"Good morning."

He jumped when he noticed her.

"I'm sorry. Didn't mean to scare you." She blushed.

"It's all right." Xavier put the knife down on the counter. "You didn't scare me."

"Good." She moved toward him. She rarely instigated lovemaking unless they were in bed, but today she was leaving her inhibitions at the door. She pressed herself against him suggestively. She caressed his chest, abdomen, lowered her head to flick her tongue across his nipples, and tasted him like she wanted.

Xavier took the hint. His hot palms cupped both sides of her face and drew her upward, and before she knew it, he was lifting the hem of the T-shirt over her head and she was standing naked in front of him. But this wasn't about her. It was about him. She dropped to her knees and shoved his swim shorts down his legs so she could take his length in her hands. She worshipped him with her mouth and tongue, rhythmically using heat and suction so she could take him all the way over the edge. She felt his surrender when his hands tangled in her hair, and he cried out her name.

Afterward, she glanced up at him and licked her lips.

"Damn, Porscha!" He helped her up, then gripped her by the waist and lifted her up onto the countertop. "Now it's my turn."

His hands moved downward to the place where she was already wet and damp, to give all the pleasure she could bear. Porscha lost herself to the delight of Xavier thrusting his fingers inside her. And when he opened his mouth over her neck and sucked, she gasped, clenching around his fingers. While she was still quivering, he put on protection from his shorts' pocket and drove deep inside in her slick heat.

Porscha twined her arms around his shoulders and when she glanced at him, she found they were eye to eye. Man and woman. Hard and soft.

"Hold on to me," Xavier rasped, and she closed her legs around his waist.

Then he began moving, withdrawing and returning. He would thrust in deep and hold her there, suspended for a moment, before dragging out slowly. He aroused her with each thrust until the tempo began to build. Porscha couldn't turn away from his watchful gaze. Soon she was flying apart, and he was right there, too. Her heart raced along with his, and time and space swirled in an epic moment that left them both shattered and shouting each other's names.

* * *

Xavier stared out at the ocean from the open door of the living room terrace while Porscha slept in the other room. He liked coming here to Turks and Caicos. He'd found this place soothing when he'd been looking for a retreat after his injury. It gave him a calm he desperately needed at the time. He hoped bringing Porscha here would do the same for her.

Instead, once again he felt out of control and was looking for something to hold on to. He wasn't a weak or needy man when it came to women, but Porscha was a habit he'd become addicted to.

She was a sexy goddess, and he was unable to resist her. And it wasn't just physically. When she'd come to him in Atlanta crying for help, Xavier had nearly lost his mind. He'd been angry at those who betrayed her and fiercely protective, ready to fight anyone who might harm her. He didn't want to love her, wasn't even sure he understood what those feelings might look like, but he knew something had changed between them. Somehow, he'd left the vault door open and forgot to check the lock on his heart. And Porscha had become an expert safecracker who intuitively knew how to turn the padlock.

It was why he wasn't in bed with her now. The intense feelings he felt scared him. He and Porscha didn't have the best track record. Nearly four years ago, he'd screwed things up royally when he'd been afraid to acknowledge what was between them. Fast-forward, and Porscha was in the driver's seat, telling him she only wanted to scratch an itch and have a secret affair.

Now, here they were, months later, and the itch

hadn't been scratched. It wasn't unusual for them to make love two or three times a day when they were together. Sometimes it was hot and fast, other times it was slow and sexy. Today was no exception, because after he'd made love to her on the kitchen counter, they'd gone back to the bedroom and immersed themselves in each other.

They had ignored their phones when they rang and beeped, and then turned them off. They ignored the growl of their stomachs and instead feasted on each other until they were a tangled, exhausted heap of limbs on the bed and all he could hear was the panting of their breaths and hearts beating in unison.

It was heady stuff, and Xavier took a shower and escaped from the bedroom because he realized he could be half in love with a woman he wasn't entirely sure of. Was he good enough for her? Although Porscha had explained she'd only dated Ryan for her career, he couldn't help but wonder if she wanted Xavier for himself? Or was he just a distraction? An escape from the drudgery of her famous lifestyle? Would accepting the top anchor position at ASN be enough to keep her?

He felt a presence behind him seconds before he felt the tips of Porscha's breasts against his back. She was naked.

Damn her.

"Xavier? Is everything okay?"

He nodded. "Yeah."

She slid around to face him and caressed both sides of his face. "Are you sure?" She searched his face, and he did his best to hide his inner turmoil.

Could she sense his unease at the feelings he just

discovered? "Of course. But I am a bit hungry. You've exhausted me, woman."

She blushed and lowered her head. "So am I. I believe I thwarted your earlier attempts at making breakfast."

"I'm not complaining," Xavier said with a bemused smile, "but I do think we need to feed our bodies. You go shower and I'll have something rustled up by the time you're out."

She rose on her tippy-toes to brush a kiss across his lips.

"If I haven't told you already, you're amazing." Then she padded away, and Xavier couldn't help but watch her naked bottom as she departed.

Had she imagined the wary look in Xavier's eyes? Porscha wondered as she showered underneath the rain showerhead in the master bath several minutes later. There had been something in Xavier's stance as he stood staring out at the sea that made her nervous.

Was he regretting bringing her here?

He shared with her in bed how this was his happy place. The place he came to for peace, quiet and clarity. Did her coming with him change that? She knew she had a lot of baggage. And she was attracting a slew of unwanted attention. It was why when she'd first set out for Atlanta yesterday, she'd switched cars with Jose, dressed in some of Erin's old clothes, worn a wig and flown coach. She hadn't wanted anyone to recognize her.

It had worked. She'd arrived at the airport in Atlanta with the press being none the wiser, but for how long?

Erin knew about her arrangement with Xavier. Would she tell the press about that, too?

And was *arrangement* the right word? In Porscha's mind it was a relationship. But did he feel the same way? Was that why he was uneasy—because he feared she would want more than he was able to give? They'd only discussed exclusivity in the terms of being bed partners, but never anything more.

Porscha didn't want to be with any other man, in or out of bed. Xavier was *her man*. Whenever she was around him, he overloaded her senses and made her knees weak. Over all these months, she'd sought refuge in her work hoping it would cure her of her infatuation with him, but it hadn't. The feelings had only grown stronger. It was why she'd told Ryan the truth—that she couldn't fake-date him.

But how did Xavier feel? She hoped this time together would not only bring her clarity about what to do next with her career, but clarity on what to do about Xavier the man she'd fallen in love with.

"Want some company?" Porscha asked Xavier when she found him outside laid out on the terrace watching the sunset later that evening. He had finished dinner and it was warming on the stove.

"Of course." He patted the lounger beside him. "Have a seat."

When she did, he caught a whiff of her floral scent. She'd changed into one of his T-shirts and shorts that he'd left out for her while she showered. When Porscha arrived at his parents' place in Atlanta, she'd come with nothing. He realized then how much she must have needed to escape, if she didn't even have time to pack a bag.

"It's nice here," Porscha said, leaning back to enjoy the view. "I can see why you come."

"It's my happy place, but it's even better now that you're here."

She turned sideways to face him. "Do you really mean that?"

"I do. Listen, Porscha," Xavier began. "I need to know what we're doing here."

"What are you asking me?"

Xavier chuckled. He'd heard these words before from women he'd been dating, but now the shoe was on the other foot. "You know what I mean. We've been skating around this topic, but if I need to be the one to put my cards on the table first, then fine, I'll do it. I know I said I wanted exclusivity before, and I think you interpreted that as us just sleeping together."

"I did."

"I don't want us to be just exclusive bed buddies," Xavier said, glancing into her light brown eyes. "I want more. I want to see where this—" he pointed back and forth between them "—goes outside the bedroom." He knew every man around the world licked his lips in lascivious heat over Porscha and the image she presented, but he wanted them to know she was his and his alone.

"Are you saying you want a relationship?" Porscha asked.

"That's exactly what I'm saying."

"Then the answer is yes," Porscha said, hopping up from the lounger and tackling him. Xavier captured her mouth in a firm, hungry kiss and Porscha returned his passion. He grunted and his hands went low to her back, pressing her bottom and pulling her tighter against him. She didn't protest. She merely shoved herself closer.

The kiss was explosive, with each of them flicking their tongue back and forth across the other. A wash of delirious pleasure overtook Xavier. He wanted to cover her, push inside her, and take them both to a place where nothing and no one could touch them. He lifted his head and cupped her face as he looked into her eyes.

"You know this changes everything," Xavier said when she moved backward and they were eye to eye. "I won't share you with other men."

"And I won't share you with other women," Porscha returned. "You're mine."

Xavier smiled. "I've only been in a meaningful relationship once before, and it was years ago."

"Will you tell me about it?" Porscha asked.

He nodded. Only his family knew what happened in college because he never shared it with anyone else, but he felt comfortable enough with Porscha now. "Her name was Tyra. We dated while I was in my senior year in college. She wanted to get serious, but I was up for a Heisman, so all of my energy went to football. Tyra was angry. To get back at me, she slept with other players and when she fell pregnant, she claimed I was the father."

"What happened?"

"Her lies threatened to derail my professional football chances and my dad wasn't having it. He had our private investigator look into it. He discovered the truth."

"So you know what it's like to be lied to, to be betrayed," Porscha said.

"I do. It's why my relationships became transient and I put my career before everything else. But I don't want to do that this time. I want to get to know you better. I want you to believe in me again. Like you did in Denver."

Her brows furrowed in consternation. "I do believe in you, Xavier. I wouldn't have come to you if I didn't. I want a relationship with you, too. I was afraid to ask for it because I thought you only wanted me physically."

"Although I enjoy making love with you, Porscha," Xavier said, "you're more than just your looks and your body."

"For so long, in my personal and professional life, it's always been about my appearances," Porscha responded, "so it's been hard to separate what's real and what isn't. But as time went on with you, I've come to realize you are the person I met in Denver on those longs walks on the mountain trails. I judged you too harshly back then because of my own insecurities. I want to wipe the slate clean. Can we have a fresh start?"

Xavier felt like he had waited forever for Porscha to say those words, but she finally had and he was thrilled. "Yes, we can."

Fifteen

After telling her mother she wouldn't be returning to Los Angeles until the movie restarted, Porscha spent an idyllic several days with Xavier on the island. She knew Diane wasn't happy with her, but she didn't care. She ignored her mother's repeated calls and texts. For the longest time, she'd listened to her advice, but it was time for Porscha to make her own decisions about what was right for her. Right now, she needed peace of mind and she got it in Turks and Caicos. There were long lazy days spent swimming in the ocean, sunbathing by the pool, writing lyrics for new songs or eating one of the Creole dishes Xavier liked to cook. Then there were the passion-filled nights spent wrapped up in each other's arms. But more than that, there was companionship, an ease they had found with each other.

They laughed and talked about their favorite films or music. In Xavier's case, Porscha discovered he loved classical, which she had never known. It was what they were listening to now as they sat on the beach on a blanket underneath the stars, sipping wine Xavier had gotten delivered earlier that day, along with a slew of groceries and other things. He'd had no idea she liked country music and that she would love to sing a duet with one of the popular stars in country music.

"Country?" Xavier quirked a brow. "I would never have guessed. Why haven't you tried to record a song?"

Porscha sighed. "Why do you think? Between my mother and my record label, they don't think it goes with my brand."

"That's bull. You should sing what feels right to you."

"That's easier said than done. You know my mother."

"I do, but you have to put your foot down, Porsch. You can't let her run your life. You're the one putting yourself out there day after day, night after night. I've seen your grueling work schedule. There's no time for you to rest."

"It's why the last few days have been so idyllic," Porscha said. "I know I have to go back to the real world and face whatever is being said about me, but I've enjoyed this respite to just breathe and be me. And that's because of you. You give me the space and freedom to be completely free."

"I feel the same way," Xavier said. "As much as I tried to act like your bed buddy, it was never just about sex for me."

"No? I rather thought you enjoyed that part." She gave him a saucy smirk.

A large grin spread across Xavier's features. "I did. And I do. Talking with you gave me the courage to mentor the Atlanta Cougars players."

"I only encouraged you to do what was in your heart."

"How would you feel if I went back to football?"

"How so?" She remembered from the clinic that his injury was too substantial for him to ever play again.

"My father keeps offering me an assistant coach position."

"I thought you decided to stay where you were."

Xavier shrugged. "I admit there's a certain freedom I have being on television, especially when the season is over."

"Is that when you do your work at the Lockett Foundation? How would that work if you coached?"

"It would be hard to juggle," Xavier answered honestly. "Even though there's an off-season, you don't get much time to yourself because you have to get the players ready for the next season. It's been four years since I had to live my life by that kind of rigorous schedule. I'm not sure I want to go back. And I don't want to put our relationship under any kind of pressure because of my schedule."

Porscha shook her head. "As much as I appreciate you putting us first, I want you to do something you *love*. That you're passionate about. Whatever *that* is, we'll make it work."

Xavier leaned over and brushed his lips tenderly across hers. "Thank you."

"For what?"

"For being you and not pressuring me either way. My father has been so insistent that getting back into football is the right thing, but I've hesitated."

"Because your heart isn't in it anymore?" Porscha offered.

He nodded. "I think I've found my purpose with the Lockett Foundation and mentoring others. And now ASN is offering me a top anchor position. It would not only be a high-profile position, but a platform to help raise awareness for my charities while still allowing me a glimpse of the sport I love."

"Then maybe that's your answer."

Xavier stared at her, but she knew he wasn't thinking of her in that moment. He was probably figuring out his next step. Porscha was simply happy that he wanted her opinion in his decision-making process. *This* was the relationship she always wanted, but never thought she'd have.

Xavier was amazed at how being with Porscha away from all the noise and the distractions brought him the clarity he'd been searching for. Was it because his walls had come down and they both admitted they wanted a relationship?

Knowing Porscha felt the same way had been a surprise to him. When he went backstage all those months ago after hearing her sing the national anthem, Porscha had been so angry with him. He never thought it was possible to get back what they had in Denver, but they'd come full circle, as if *this* was where they were always supposed to be.

He reached for a tendril of her hair that was flying in the breeze and tucked it behind her ear. "You're pretty amazing, do you know that?"

"Me?" She shrugged. "I'm nothing special. Don't believe the hype."

"Don't say that. Because you are. You're special to me," Xavier said, caressing her cheek. "You always put yourself down. Why do you do that?"

"I don't know."

But he knew she was lying. She was covering up her feelings because they were uncomfortable to talk about. But she'd just helped him make a breakthrough about a big decision. He wanted to help her. "You can tell me anything."

"Tell you what?" Porscha asked. "That every day when I'm out there singing, I'm waiting for the other shoe to drop? Waiting for everyone to realize I'm a fraud and don't deserve to be there? You mean that?"

"Why would you feel that way? You're super talented."

"Because there's always someone telling me I'm never quite good enough—that I have to work out a little bit harder. Practice dancing a little bit longer. Eat a little bit less. Get bigger boobs. Sometimes it's like I can't do anything right and I feel like I'm on a never-ending treadmill with no destination insight."

"Who makes you feel this way?"

"My mother. My record label. The public. My ex-boyfriend."

"Tell me about him," Xavier said.

She shook her head. "Why? He's long gone. He got what he wanted, and it was on to the next meal ticket."

"He's obviously not gone if you're still holding on to the hurt." He wanted to be there for Porscha like she was there for him when he told her about Tyra.

She regarded him and then looked back into the dark night. Xavier thought she wasn't going to share her feelings, but then she began speaking. "I met Gil when I was twenty and working on my first demo," Porscha said. "I had never been in love and Gil was older. He was good-looking and charming. Oh, so charming. And I fell for him *hard*."

"What happened?"

"I was discovered by my record label. Fame came instantly along with the accolades for my first album. I was giddy with excitement, but the more successful I became, the angrier Gil got. Even though during every interview, I said I owed my success to him for always being in my corner. That wasn't enough for Gil. He didn't like being the man on the side. He wanted to be front and center because he's a narcissist."

"Some men can't accept their woman being more successful than they are."

Porscha nodded. "He was definitely one of those. He sold my story to a tabloid that paid him thousands of dollars to talk about what a spoiled diva I was. He even threatened to publish pictures of me that were for his eyes only, if I didn't pay him off."

"What did you do?"

"I paid him." Xavier could see the pain Porscha felt as she relived the story. A single tear trickled down her cheek, which she quickly brushed away with the back of her hand. "He threatened my career and the clean-cut image my record label had established for me. I couldn't let him do that. I had to shut him down before he parlayed his five minutes of fame into fifteen."

"I'm sorry, baby." Xavier scooted closer to her. "That's terrible. You should never have had to endure something like that."

"I suppose that's why I flipped out in the clinic, when I thought you, too, were using me. It was a trigger and made me think that yet again I'd fallen for the wrong man."

"I was trying to protect your privacy and instead made the situation worse. I caused you to doubt *me*."

Porscha reached across the distance and stroked his cheek. "I don't doubt you, Xavier, not anymore." And to prove it, she moved forward and their mouths met in a searing kiss right before they fell back on the sand in a tangle of limbs. Xavier wanted Porscha like he'd never wanted any other woman. He didn't stop kissing her. He couldn't. She inhabited him completely, not just in body, but in mind and soul.

Xavier's hands were everywhere, clenching in her hair, stroking her back and molding her breasts, but his mouth never left hers and she wouldn't want it to. Every inch of Porscha's skin heated as it came into contact with his tall, powerful body. And the scent of him filled her head, electrifying her senses. By the time his fingers brushed against her taut nipple in the polka dot bikini she wore, her back arched, craving for a deeper touch.

She looked up at him and found herself staring into his dark brown eyes fringed with long lashes. He always managed to hold her in her thrall. She tore at his

T-shirt, lifting it up and over his head so she could run her palms along his hair-roughened chest. She reveled in his hot skin and sculpted muscles.

Xavier's breath came out in a hiss. "I want to feel your skin on mine," he told her and then he was reaching behind her to untie her bikini top and bare her breasts to his incendiary gaze. Then he bent his head and his mouth touched her everywhere his hands had been. He left her senses spinning with every nibble and suckle of his lips.

Porscha clutched his head to her, sobbing in pleasure as he tasted her, but she needed more. Xavier intuitively understood, because his fingers were deftly finding and stroking her over her bikini bottoms.

"Please... Xavier."

He gave her what she needed by untying the damp fabric and plunging two fingers inside her. The pleasure was so acute that Porscha gasped. She reached for his shorts, fumbling to push them down.

"Porscha, I need..."

As hungry as she was, she appreciated Xavier being responsible and when he moved away for a few seconds and returned fully protected, she parted her legs. His invasion was swift, but so sweet. Tears stung Porscha's eyes because she wasn't just giving Xavier her body, she was giving him her love. Every time he caressed her, her carefully guarded heart became undone.

She wrapped her legs around him, taking him even deeper inside her. Xavier reached for her hands, placing them above her head and entwining them with his, then started to move faster. Porscha matched his rhythm and with each thrust, her body responded, opening up to him like a flower. Dizzying pleasure filled her, and she began climbing to a far-off summit.

Porscha thought she wouldn't reach it until Xavier brought his hand between their rocking bodies and intimately caressed her with his clever fingers and sent her into a free fall.

"Xavier!" She called out his name and he called out hers as his climax rushed over him and their bodies shuddered in tandem. In the aftermath, Porscha lay there, Xavier's body on top of hers, and she realized she could stay here in this moment with him forever.

Sixteen

Forever proved to be a fantasy because the next morning, reality came roaring back.

After making love on the beach the previous night, they'd come back to the house, showered and fallen asleep in each other's arms. It felt so good until the morning called and Porscha awoke.

The memory of how honest and truthful they had been was a turning point in their relationship. Porscha had shared things with Xavier no one else knew, not Erin and not even her mother. With Xavier, she felt safe enough to reveal her deepest thoughts and fears. He hadn't judged her or told her she was wrong. He listened and allowed Porscha to see that she needed to make some changes in her life.

It wasn't going to be easy.

Walking naked to the kitchen, Porscha began making coffee.

She'd been in a rut for far too long allowing everyone else to tell her how to live her life, but that was over. She needed to live her life *for her*. Doing what made Porscha happy. Because at the end of the day, *she* was worth it.

Once the coffee was brewed, she poured her and Xavier a cup and went to the bedroom with the steaming mugs. Xavier was still sleeping soundly, so she left his cup on the nightstand. She would have walked out naked on the terrace but saw Xavier's robe lying at the edge of the bed. She slid it on, not bothering to tie it. Instead, she left it open because theirs was a private beach. They'd had complete privacy all week.

She walked outside on the terrace and within seconds was greeted by camera flashes as paparazzi took pictures of her from every angle. The coffee cup she'd been holding flew out of her hands and crashed to the terrace floor.

"Porscha! Have long have you been hiding out with Xavier Lockett?"

"Is he the reason you dumped Ryan Mills?"

Porscha was frozen and unable to move as she stared at the crowd of reporters and camera crew on the sand.

Xavier must have heard the crash, because he was behind her within seconds, closing her robe and leading her back inside the bedroom. He slammed the door shut.

How much had they seen of her?

"It's okay, baby. I've got you."

"How did they find us?" Porscha asked, sitting down

on the bed. They'd been so careful all week. They'd never gone out.

"I don't know." Xavier scrubbed his hand across his beard and began pacing the floor.

The only time they'd seen anyone was when the delivery driver dropped off the wine, food and the few items of clothing Xavier purchased for her during the trip. He had to have told the press.

"It was the delivery guy," Porscha said. "He must have recognized me. Oh, Lord!" She rolled her eyes upward. "How are we going to get out of this?"

"Get out of what?" Xavier said, turning to face Porscha. "There's nothing to get out of. Listen, baby—" he crouched down in front of her "—we haven't done anything wrong. There's nothing to be ashamed of."

"They caught me outside half-dressed," Porscha replied, her voice rising.

"Yes, you were a bit compromised, but it's not that bad, Porscha. You were clothed."

"But I looked thoroughly tumbled. As if I just rolled out of your bed after a night of hot sex."

Xavier smiled at the memory of Porscha on top of him as she'd ridden him hard and fast. "It *was* hot."

"Don't be cute," Porscha replied, rushing to her feet and pacing the floor. "The press will crucify me. If they haven't already." She left the room and Xavier followed behind her to see her grab her purse. She pulled out her cell phone, which she hadn't touched the entire time they'd been on the island, and turned it on.

He heard beeps as her messages and voice mails filtered in, followed by her audible gasps. "Is it bad?"

"The press thinks I've gone off the deep end, and add highly sexed-up, once those pictures of me in your robe surface," Porscha said bluntly.

Xavier reminded himself that he was new to her world and that Porscha needed his patience, not his ire.

"Whatever comes, we'll handle it together," he assured her, taking in her forlorn expression. "As long as we go out there together and publicly acknowledge we're a couple, it'll blow over. Maybe even spin this to our advantage. My sister-in-law Elyse is in publicity. Last year, when our most popular player, Curtis, got in a bit of trouble, she was there to bail him out. His reputation remains untarnished. I'm sure she can help us."

"That's easy for you to say, Xavier. You haven't been in my position. You don't know what kind of vultures they can be."

"Maybe not the same as you, but when I injured my knee, the press was terrible. There was no amount of optics to fix the fact I was never going to walk the same or be able to play football."

"I know and I'm sorry, honey." Porscha came rushing toward him and touched his arm. "I know you've had your share of tussles with the press. I just don't know if I can deal with any more drama. First the Gil incident, then when my second album bombed and the truth about my mental breakdown. Now this."

"What's so bad about being with me?" Xavier replied. He couldn't understand why she was making a mountain out of a molehill about the press discovering their relationship.

"Nothing. I… I just wasn't ready to put our relationship out there for public consumption. I wanted it to be between the two of us."

"So you want to keep us a secret?"

She shook her head. "No, it's not like that, Xavier. I just need to get back home and figure out my next move."

"What is it like, Porscha?" Xavier wondered aloud. "Here I am asking you to stay here with me so we can figure this out together, but you're ready to run back to Los Angeles with your tail between your legs. I don't get what's happening here."

"I need to call my mother." And without another word, she turned and rushed to the bathroom, closing the door.

"Do you have any idea what you've done?" her mother railed on the other end of the phone at Porscha as she wore a hole in the tile floor.

"I'm not a child, Mama, so don't talk down to me like I'm one. I took some much-needed time off after someone I trusted betrayed me," Porscha responded.

"So what if Erin said you'd been at a mental health facility? Celebrities have breakdowns all the time. We could have spun it, but this? Going off and gallivanting with that Lockett boy? The press is labeling you a cheat."

"A cheat?" Porscha asked, confused. "On who?"

"On Ryan!" her mother yelled. "We were setting it up to look like the two of you were headed for super-couple-dom and you've gone and blown it up. You're trending, but not in a good way."

Porscha sighed. "I should never have agreed to go along with that charade in the first place."

"Are you blaming me for this mess? I'm not the one that was just caught half-naked coming from some strange man's bed."

"Mama! That's enough," Porscha hissed. "I will not have you talk about Xavier like he's some random hookup, because he's not."

"Fine. What do you want to do?"

"Oh, I get to choose?" Porscha asked tightly. Usually, her mother—and everyone else for that matter—was telling her what to do, how to look, what to eat, every single minute of every single day. The last week had been a breath of fresh air.

"Don't be smart, Porscha."

"Well, I choose to stay here with Xavier. We'll walk out together and when we're ready we'll issue a joint statement."

"Do you really think that's wise?" her mother asked. "You haven't even been seen with Xavier. The press think you and Ryan were an item. Now all of sudden you're leaving hand in hand as lovers? The media already has doubts about your mental health, and now they'll call you a cheat. Don't stoke the flames. Come home alone."

"I don't know." Porscha didn't want to leave Xavier. Not like this. Their relationship was still so new, so fresh. It needed to be nurtured.

"Trust me, Porscha. Have I ever steered you wrong?"

"Other than with Ryan, no, you haven't," Porscha admitted, but that didn't mean this wasn't the exception.

"I've already called a private plane service. A driver

and bodyguard will be there to pick you up within a half hour to bring you back to the States. They need you back on the film anyway."

"Fine."

"And, Porscha? Please do something with yourself," her mother said. "From the candid, I saw your hair is a mess, and you didn't have on a lick of makeup."

Porscha ended the call. She hadn't needed makeup because Xavier liked her just the way she was. She glanced at the door. She wasn't looking forward to what she had to do next, but there was no way around it. She had to tell Xavier she was leaving *without him*.

Xavier could hear Porscha in the bathroom talking to Diane, but he couldn't make out what they were saying. Eventually, the call must have ended because he heard the shower. What was going on? Why hadn't she come out to talk to him, to tell him where her head was? He thought they were in this together. They'd agreed to work on their relationship, but at the first test, Porscha seemed to be getting cold feet.

When she finally returned to the living room fifteen minutes later, she was wearing one of the summer dresses he'd purchased on the island for her. Her long hair had been swept up into a simple knot and her normally bare face held lipstick and, if he wasn't mistaken, some mascara. He liked Porscha's bare face. She was not only beautiful without all the adornments, but it showed she trusted him enough to be real with him, flaws and all. Not that she had any.

"Porscha?"

She looked down at the floor and when she gazed

back up at him there were tears in her eyes. "I have to go."

"Have to?" Xavier asked, raising a brow. "I don't think so."

"Xavier, please understand that I need to go home. Everything's a mess and I have to strategize on what to do next and how not to make a mockery of my budding acting career, not to mention the singing career I've worked so hard to build."

"I get that, Porscha," Xavier said, coming toward her and taking both her hands in his. "I do. But why can't we do that together? I thought we agreed to have a relationship, and if we're doing that, you have to make space for me. I'm asking you to publicly acknowledge what's between us so we can walk out of this house united."

He wanted her to show him how she felt about him. Show him he was worth it, worth fighting for.

"And I will," Porscha said. "But not now. I don't want to add fuel to the fire. The press is all over me right now about Ryan and the mental breakdown. Let me just get back home and once this dies down, we can come out as a couple."

"So you're refusing to tell everyone we're together?" Xavier pressed. "Are you embarrassed to be seen with me?" He knew he wasn't Ryan Mills, but he also thought they'd made progress in their relationship.

"Of course not."

"Then why won't you publicly commit to me?" Xavier asked. "Why won't you tell the media out there—" he pointed toward the door "—that I'm your man. That you're here with me because you want to be."

"I can't comment about us right now. It's bad timing. I was just now dating Ryan. How would it look if I said I was with you instead? The public already think I'm flighty and a complete mess. Please let me do this *alone*."

"Fine," Xavier said. "Go out there alone as if the last week, hell, all these months with me meant nothing. I'm just the man you've been sleeping with, after all, and in the eyes of the public and apparently you, I'm not good enough to be seen with."

"You're deliberately misunderstanding me and making this all about you."

"When has it ever been about me?" Xavier shouted. "The one time I ask you to do something *for me*. To show me *you care*. God." He turned away because he couldn't face her. "I don't know why I'm fighting so hard for a relationship that's obviously not important to you."

"If it wasn't important to me, I wouldn't have flown to Atlanta after my date with Ryan to make things right between us. I wouldn't have stayed here with you this past week." The doorbell rang and Porscha glanced at the front door. "I have to go."

"Of course, you do," Xavier said. "But just know, I won't be waiting for you anymore."

"What's that's supposed to mean?"

The doorbell rang again. This time a little bit more insistently.

"It means it's over between us, Porscha. I'm tired of fighting for us. I'm tired of being the one constantly giving and getting nothing in return." When she began to speak, he interrupted her. "And I'm not talking about sex. We've always had a problem with communication and apparently that hasn't changed."

The bell rang a third time and this time Porscha began walking toward the door. "I'm sorry you feel that way, Xavier. I've given you all that I'm able to right now. I'm sorry if it's not enough for you."

Seconds later, she closed the door, leaving him alone.

Xavier was angry. Angry that Porscha had left him again. Why was she the one always doing the leaving? It was just like Denver. She hadn't stayed to hear what he had to say back then, either. Except this time, there was a difference. This time he was in love, and the woman he adored had walked out on him and hadn't looked back.

Seventeen

"Can I get you anything, Ms. Childs?" the stewardess asked Porscha on the flight back to Los Angeles.

Porscha shook her head. "No, not right now." As much as she wanted a stiff drink, nothing would ease the pain she felt right now.

Xavier had ended their relationship.

She was sitting on the plush reclining chair in utter disbelief. She didn't care that her mother had sent a luxurious private jet to retrieve her, or that it had every amenity Porscha could need—from a stewardess serving drinks and light snacks, to a private bedroom in the rear with its own master bath.

None of it mattered because she wasn't here with the man she loved. It was true: she loved Xavier. The minute she pulled away from their beautiful island retreat, she'd known she wasn't just falling in love, she was *in love* with Xavier. With his smile. With his warmth. With the way he made her feel. The way he made her feel beautiful, safe and protected.

But had it been real?

Or had she created a world in her mind because she desperately needed something to believe in after the betrayals she'd endured. All she asked for, all she needed from him, was a little patience, so she could figure out her next move. The entertainment world was so fickle. She couldn't react and think about the consequences later. She'd done that when she fled to Atlanta and to Turks and Caicos.

And Xavier had taken her in. Comforted her. Assured her it was going to be all right. And maybe it would be, but she had to start doing things on her own. Porscha knew it was selfish of her to not include Xavier in this journey, but she had rediscovered herself on that island. Learned she was strong and resilient and would make it through this snafu like she'd done all the rest.

The only difference was she would be doing it on *her* terms. She'd made some decisions while she'd sat on the beach day after day with Xavier. And as soon as she returned to Los Angeles, she intended to implement them, but first she had to get all her ducks in a row. Once they were, somehow, someway, she would get her man back.

"Appreciate the ride, big sis," Xavier said when Giana picked him up from the airport later that evening. Once Porscha had left, Xavier couldn't stay in the house anymore. Because memories of her and the two of them together haunted him and it was no longer his happy place. It was a place where relationships came to die, and he would never go there again.

Leaving had been problematic. Hordes of press had been waiting for him to leave the villa, snapping pictures and throwing out questions and comments about him and Porscha. He refused to answer them and instead slid into the town car and headed to the airport. Though there was a handful of reporters there, he'd evaded them, making it off the island without further incident.

"Of course," Giana replied. "When you told me what happened, I was angry. Angry that you were by yourself, and I wasn't able to be there for you. But I am now."

"I'm a big boy, Gigi. I can take care of myself."

"Yes, you can," Giana stated evenly, returning her eyes to the road. "But you will always be my little brother. And if I want to be angry with the woman who hurt you, then let me."

"It was my own fault," Xavier responded. "I think I was starting to believe all the hype. Probably came from hanging around you and my brothers lately. Must be something in the air."

Giana chuckled. "I don't think you *catch* love."

"Who said anything about love?" Xavier countered. He didn't even want to think about the word ever again, because if this was what it felt like, his siblings could have it. He wanted no part of this heartache.

"You didn't have to," Giana said. "I have two eyes." She glanced over in his direction. "And they see a man hurting because the woman he loves walked out on him."

"You don't know what you're talking about."

"Like hell I don't," she responded fiercely. "I know because I've been where you are, Xavier. Don't you remember me crying on your shoulder when Wynn thought I'd betrayed him—with Blaine Smith, of all people. I can't stand that guy."

Xavier nodded. "Yeah, I recall."

"So, then you also can't forget who was there to comfort me," she returned.

He smiled and looked warmly at her. "No. I haven't." He, Roman and Julian had been ready to string Wynn up by his shoelaces and beat him to a bloody pulp. It was only because they promised Giana they'd leave him alone that his future brother-in-law still had his teeth.

"Good, because I'm returning the favor," Giana replied. "I'm not taking you back to the guesthouse, where you will be alone to brood like Lockett men do. I'm taking you back to my place."

"Giana…"

"Don't whine, Xavier, because it may have worked with me when you were eight years old, but it's not going to work on me now."

Xavier laughed. When he was younger, he'd always made big puppy dog eyes at her and she would give him whatever he wanted. "I don't want to cramp your and Wynn's style. You're nearly newlyweds."

"Not until this summer," Giana said with a grin. "Because Mama has to have her big wedding. And as for cramping our style, you will have an entire wing of the house to yourself."

"All right." Xavier didn't have it in him to fight. He went along with Giana's request and let his big sister flutter around him, from getting him settled in the guest wing, to making one of her vegetarian concoctions. He was happy when the day ended, and he could shuffle off to bed and sulk.

Giana was right.

He was angry.

Angry at Porscha.

Angry at himself.

He should never have allowed himself to fall in love. He'd seen the train wreck coming, especially when he found himself wanting to cook for Porscha and show her they were more than just sex. But had he heeded the warning? No. Instead, he'd walked headfirst into disaster, and he only had himself to blame, because he had allowed his feelings of tenderness for Porscha to grow from lust. He hadn't kept this heart locked. He'd left the door open and Porscha had entered. Or perhaps love had always been there from years ago?

Xavier didn't know. All he was left with was the memories and they came by the truckload. Flooding his body and his mind with all the places he'd touched her, kissed her, made love to her. And there had been some interesting places. Her dressing room the night she sang the national anthem. A broom closet during one of her shows. She'd flown him up for the show, but she'd been so tense he'd known of only one way to ease it.

Afterward, she'd been relaxed, and the concert had been killer. Then there was the time they became part of the mile-high club. Porscha had sat on his lap and given Xavier the best ride of his life. Then there was the villa in Turks and Caicos where they'd made love all day and all night until their empty stomachs growled in protest.

Xavier could feel himself getting hard as images of Porscha's face, her smile, her incredible body and her amazing voice flashed through his head. It seemed like they were on an interminable loop that he couldn't stop. Slamming the pillow over his head, he prayed for sleep because the morning couldn't come soon enough.

"Well, if it isn't the diva herself," Ryan said when Porscha joined him on set the following day.

"Did you enjoy your jaunt down to the Caribbean?"

"First of all, don't be a brat, Ryan," Porscha responded. At his frown, she amended her words. "Don't be so sensitive, it was a joke. Seriously though, I had a great time in Turks and Caicos, thank you very much. Perhaps you should try it. Maybe you'd be more relaxed."

Ryan stared at her for several beats and then burst out laughing. "I like you, Porscha. You give as good as you get. And you're going to need that in show business."

"This isn't my first rodeo."

"No, but Hollywood is. It helps to have a friend. And I can be a friend or a foe."

Porscha was going to take his advice. "Well, then, Ryan." She leaned toward him. "How about you give me some advice about changing managers."

His brow rose. "You would fire your mom?"

"Quite frankly, it's long overdue," Porscha responded. "It's time I start doing things *my way*."

Ryan reached into the pocket of his button-down shirt and pulled out a business card. "Call my manager. He only reps the best and if I vouch for you, you're in."

Porscha smiled. "Thank you."

"I think you've got talent, Porscha, and not just to be a singer. You can be a breakout star, the next Jennifer Hudson, but don't tell anyone I told you so."

Porscha laughed and pinched her index finger and thumb together and ran them across her mouth. "My lips are sealed."

Later that day, after Ryan arranged for Porscha to meet with his manager and after they came to a hand-shake agreement, she returned home and went to her safe to retrieve the contract she had with her mother. She took it to her room and settled in on the bed to read it.

There was a provision for a thirty-day termination without cause, but her mother would receive a payout for any deals Porscha had in progress that were signed during her mother's tenure.

For some time, Porscha had known it was necessary to end their business relationship. It was the only way they would ever get back to being mother and daughter. Because right now, Porscha had it up to here with her mother as her manager.

It wasn't long before her mother came knocking on her door. Diane wasted no time giving her another lecture for leaving without notifying her.

"You're not my keeper," Porscha responded.

"No. I'm your manager and when you disappear

without a word, I have to deal with it. You had several appointments that needed to be rescheduled."

"I'm sorry, it couldn't be avoided."

"Because you were with that Lockett boy?" her mother asked.

"He's not a boy. He's a man."

"Yes, I know," her mother responded tightly. "I just don't think he's the right man for you. With your looks and your talent, you can have any man in the world, but you choose a former quarterback with no future."

"That's not true. There's so much more to Xavier than how famous he is. And I know because I've gotten to know him."

Her mother sighed. "You've always been tender-hearted, Porscha. Even when you were a little girl, you wanted to take in every stray cat and dog, but I didn't let you. Otherwise, our house would be riddled with fleas." She grabbed both of Porscha's shoulders. "Listen to me, you need to be with someone like Ryan. He's a star." Her eyes grew wide with excitement. "I'm sure if I called Ryan's people, we could smooth things over. Make it appear as if you had a lovers' tiff and are reuniting. Think of the optics."

"Stop it!" Porscha yelled, pushing away from her mother.

"What's wrong? I'm just trying to help."

"I don't need your help. I haven't needed it in a long time. I'm capable of standing on my own two feet and looking after myself, and I'm going to do that. Starting now."

"What do you mean?"

"You're fired!"

"Excuse me?" Her mother stared at her in confusion.

"You heard me. You're fired." Porscha said it louder and with more conviction. Not just for her mother, but for herself. She was putting her foot down and taking back her power.

"You can't fire me. I'm your mother."

"Oh, now you want to be my mother? When it's convenient for you?" Porscha asked, shaking her head in disbelief. "You don't get to pick and choose which role you want. You're either my mom or my manager, but you can't have both. Pick one."

"Porscha!"

"All my life I have done everything by your rules, but no more. You told me how to look, how to dress, what to eat, what to sing, how to dance. I've been your bloody puppet. Well, I won't be that person anymore."

"Where is this coming from? Xavier? Did he put you up to this?" her mother asked, staring back at her with quiet anger.

"No. He didn't. He didn't have to because I've felt this way for a long time. Because you're always pushing me. Do you know how to be a mother anymore or is it all about business with you?"

"How dare you speak to me this way after everything I've done!" Diane pointed her finger in Porscha's face. "After everything I've sacrificed to get you to this position. You wouldn't be here without me. I made you a star."

"Sacrificed?" Porscha laughed bitterly. "Well, that's a joke. I was the one in dance and singing lessons in middle school and high school. I missed out on school games, homecoming and prom because *you* told me I was destined for greatness and none of that meant anything. My entire childhood was stolen from me because I was trying to fit in the box you and my label and the whole damn world put in me. It all ends tonight!"

"Porscha, I had no idea you felt this way." Suddenly tears were slipping down her mother's cheeks. "You never said anything to me before—that you didn't want this life. All I have ever done is work hard to help you achieve your dream."

"Was it my dream, Mom?" Porscha asked, narrowing her eyes. "Or was it yours?" When her mother started to speak, she interrupted. "No, don't answer that. The choice is simple. You can bow out gracefully and pray we can have some sort of relationship in the future. Or you can keep fighting me on this, but you won't like the outcome."

"Is that a threat?"

"No, Mom. It's the facts," Porscha replied. "I don't want to lose you, but I can't keep going like this. When I went to that clinic, it was a cry for help because I was drowning. And yes, I picked myself up, but I did it because I had Xavier by my side. He helped me see the good in me and that I was special and perfect just as I am. Can you say the same?"

Her mother stared back at her in disbelief. "You're my baby girl, Porscha. I have loved you from the moment I laid eyes on you. And when your father left us, I guess I didn't know how to show you that love anymore. Instead, I put all my hopes and dreams on you. I'm sorry if you were smothered by my expectations, but I love you, Porscha. And if it's a choice being your manager and being your mother, there is no choice but one."

"I'm glad to hear you say that." Porscha hadn't been sure what her mother would choose, but it wasn't going to be easy rebuilding their relationship after years of neglect.

Diane nodded. "Thank you for giving me the chance to make things right with you."

Porscha thought about cutting all ties with her mother and making a clean break, but she did love her. She just refused to be ruled by her a second longer. "You're welcome."

"So, what do we do now?" her mother asked.

"How about we try being friends?"

"I would like that," her mother responded.

Finding her voice had helped Porscha and her mom turn a corner. And maybe someday they would have the mother-daughter relationship she'd always wanted.

Eighteen

"I'm proud of you, son," his father said after Xavier came to the Atlanta Cougars corporate headquarters and informed him he would *not* be coaching for the team.

He had a done a lot of soul-searching after Porscha left him in Turks and Caicos. She'd gutted him when she walked away, but she hadn't broken him. Xavier had given her everything he had and showed her the life they could have together. If she wasn't willing to take a risk on him, he wasn't going to wallow in it like he did when he lost football after his injury.

Xavier had already come to the realization he couldn't go back and recapture a past life. Instead, he had to embrace the man he'd become. Surprisingly, it had been Porscha who made him see that. Being a sportscaster still gave him the taste of football he loved but being a philanthropist and helping others in the Lockett Foundation and as an Atlanta Cougars mentor was his true life's work.

"You are?" Xavier said. "I thought you wanted me to coach."

"I do," his father responded, "but you have to do what's in your heart. I've tried for so long to rule your brothers and sister and get them to do things my way. But I only hurt them in the process. I don't want to do that with you. I want you to be happy, and if working at the foundation is what you love, then so be it."

"Thanks, Dad. I appreciate your support," Xavier replied. "When I came here, I was certain you were going to try and change my mind."

His father shook his head. "I won't try to sway you, but I would like to offer a piece of advice."

"About?"

"Porscha Childs."

"How much do you know?" Xavier inquired staring into his father's dark brown eyes that mirrored his own.

His father laughed. "C'mon, Xavier. There were pictures of you and the girl all over the news and social media."

"Yeah, I wasn't happy about that, either. I can't believe the press followed us all the way to the island."

"And that surprises you? Porscha Childs is big news and you're a former quarterback turned sportscaster. You're both high-profile. Nico has been keeping an eye on the situation to ensure there's no blowback on the family or the team."

Of course, his father would think of business first.

"And? I assume you have something to say about my relationship?"

"Why haven't you brought the girl around to meet the family?"

Xavier laughed. "Are you kidding me? After the reception Shantel received and your machinations with Elyse and Wynn, my siblings' significant others, that's a hell no."

"Because you don't think you have something real with her?"

"That's the thing, Dad. I do," Xavier responded. "Or at least I thought I did, but I was wrong. Porscha wants to keep our relationship hidden and out of the public eye. I think she's ashamed to be seen with me. Her mother certainly thinks so and has been pushing Ryan Mills on her."

"That actor has nothing on my son," Josiah roared. "When are you going to get it through that thick skull of yours that you haven't lost anything because you're not playing football. You're a strong, proud and caring Black man and I couldn't be prouder to have raised a son like you."

Xavier felt a broad smile spreading across his face. "Wow! I don't think I've ever heard you speak so passionately before except maybe the other day when you asked me to consider coaching again."

In his mind, Xavier had always thought he'd let his father down, but that was his own insecurity talking and not how Josiah felt. He'd said it before at the baby shower, but it hadn't really sunk in until now.

"Believe it, Xavier. You can compete with the likes of some Hollywood actor, and if Porscha Childs doesn't know that, I'm sorry for her because she's missing out on the best thing that ever happened to her."

"I didn't know I was coming for a pep talk," Xavier responded with a smile. "But I'll take it all the same."

"You're welcome. Now come here and give your father a hug."

And Xavier did just that. His father had come a long way from his boorish ways with Xavier's siblings, and he was glad to be the recipient on the other end.

"What are you still doing here?" Porscha's mother asked when filming ended a couple of weeks later and Porscha was packing up her movie trailer.

She hadn't found another personal assistant yet. It was going to take a minute for her to be able to trust someone after Erin's betrayal. She still had a tough time believing she'd gotten it so terribly wrong. So her mom was helping her out until she could find someone new.

"What did you say?" Porscha asked distractedly.

"I asked why you were still here in Los Angeles."

Porscha frowned as she glanced at her mother. "What do you mean?"

"Why aren't you in Atlanta trying to get your man back?" Over the past few weeks, on the road to getting back to a mother-daughter relationship, they had talked a great deal. One night over a cup of tea, Porscha had shared with Diane how important Xavier had been when they first met at the facility and afterward during their affair. She confided that she'd fallen in love with him.

"Why didn't you tell me how deep your feelings were for Xavier?" her mother had asked.

"If I admitted them out loud, that meant they were real, and I was so afraid of getting hurt again. This time, however, Xavier was different. He accepted the little I was willing to give him until I opened my heart to more between us. He was patient, kind and everything I've ever wanted."

"I'm sorry I misjudged him."

"You did. And I was so determined to show I could take care of myself that I turned my back on Xavier."

Now Porscha released an audible sigh. Her mom was right. As soon as the film wrapped, she should have been rushing to Atlanta, but she was afraid. Afraid of Xavier's reaction. What if he didn't forgive her for walking out of the house in Turks and Caicos without him and not telling the world they were committed to each other?

She wanted to go desperately, but she'd listened to everyone else's voice in her head for so long. It was hard to break old habits. Instead of standing by Xavier's side, she'd bolted because she'd been afraid to face her own inner demons and to let the public see the real her. She'd wanted to keep her and Xavier in a bubble where nothing and no one could hurt them, but life wasn't like that. There were going to be bumps on the road and they needed to face them together.

Yet she still hadn't called or texted him. *What could she say?*

That if she had to do it all over again, she would shout from the rooftops to anyone who would listen that she loved Xavier and couldn't live her life without him? The last couple of weeks had been misery. She'd gone to the set and back home, but she'd been unable to sing, which usually helped soothe her. And even if she could, she would sing love songs about Xavier, but she'd hurt him. She knew that. She needed to apologize and beg him to take her back.

But would he listen? Or she had she lost him forever?

There was only one way to find out. She had to go to Atlanta and try to win him back. She would have to pull out every trick in her short playbook and fight for Xavier. Make him see they had the real thing.

"You're right!" Porscha threw down the box she'd been tossing random items in and said, "I'm going to Atlanta to get my man back."

"Mama, you've outdone yourself yet again," Xavier said, rubbing his full stomach. "The meal was divine."

"I wholeheartedly concur, Angie," his father added from the head of the table, where the entire Lockett family was gathered for Sunday dinner. His mother was at the opposite end while his siblings, Roman, Julian and Giana, and their respective partners, Shantel, Elyse and Wynn, sat in the middle, along with Xavier.

His mother had cooked one of her famous Creole dishes of shrimp, chicken and andouille gumbo, and they'd all cleaned their plates and had seconds.

"You mean you don't have enough room for dessert?" his mother inquired. "I made my famous whiskey bread pudding."

"Listen, Ma," Julian said from across the table. "You know I love your food, but only one of us—" he glanced beside him to stare adoringly at his wife "—is eating for two."

Everyone laughed at the joke.

"That might be true," Elyse said, "but, Mom, even your granddaughter and I are stuffed." She patted her protruding belly. Xavier's sister-in-law was due to give birth any minute.

"Ditto on that," Giana said. "My wedding is around the corner and I have to keep this body tight."

"You have no problem in that department," Wynn said from across the table.

"Oh, Lord." Xavier rolled his eyes upward and prayed for inner strength. He couldn't bear to watch all his siblings in love with their partners while he was alone. Because the woman he loved didn't want him.

"How about we adjourn to the living room?" his mother asked. Just then the doorbell rang. "Who on earth could that be? All of you are already here."

A few seconds later, Xavier heard the click of heels on the marble floor and to his utter astonishment, Porscha stood in the doorway of the dining room. Was he imagining she was here in his family's home in Tuxedo Park?

"I was hoping there was room for one more," Porscha said, slowly walking toward him.

"And who are you, my dear?" his mother said, but his father shook his head, and she became silent as did everyone else in the room.

All eyes were on him, but Xavier couldn't move. He didn't dare, because he couldn't believe Porscha was standing in front of him. These weeks had been miserable without her. She'd become part of his DNA. He'd tried to move on as best he could, but seeing her now told him he'd failed miserably.

She looked absolutely stunning in a burgundy dress

with cap sleeves. Her hair was a simple, high ponytail, and her makeup was minimal and artless.

"I'm sorry to disturb your family dinner, Mr. and Mrs. Lockett," Porscha started. "My name is Porscha Childs, and I have been seeing your son Xavier for nearly a year, though we did know each other several years ago."

"I had no idea," his mother said softly from the other end of the table and turned to look at Xavier questioningly.

Xavier finally found his voice. "Porscha…" He didn't know what she was doing, but whatever it was, it was too late. He'd made his peace that it was over between them. He'd had to, when each day passed with no word from Porscha. And he certainly wasn't about to pick up the phone especially when he felt she'd made the wrong decision to leave him that day.

She ignored the caution in his tone. "I did Xavier a disservice and I've come here to correct that mistake."

"Yes, you did," Giana stated fiercely from across the table. "How do we know this isn't a publicity stunt?"

"Because it's not," Porscha defended herself, turning to Xavier's sister.

Xavier could tell Giana wanted to say more, but when he rose to his feet and turned to glare at her, she clammed up.

"I made him feel like he wasn't worthy of being with me, that I was ashamed of him, when that was far from the truth." Then Porscha turned her beautiful light brown eyes on him and what Xavier saw there nearly razed him to the ground. "You *are* good enough for me and I'm sorry if I made you feel otherwise. I love you,

Xavier. And I would give up the fame and the glory because all of it means nothing if I don't have you by my side. Please give me another chance to be your lady."

His father coughed loudly and just like that, everyone in the room slipped away until it was just him and Porscha standing alone in the dining room.

Xavier was afraid to move, because he was afraid to believe the words coming out of Porscha's lips. It was everything he wanted to hear but hadn't thought he ever would.

"Please tell me it's not too late," Porscha whispered. "That I haven't lost you for good."

As much as Xavier might want to deny her, he couldn't. His heart wouldn't let him. "You could never lose me, Porscha," Xavier replied. "Because I love you, too."

"You do?" Wonder was in her voice as if she hadn't been sure of his response.

"Can't you tell?" Xavier asked. "It's why I was so jealous when I found out you were dating Ryan. It's why I wanted to walk out of the house with you on my arm in Turks and Caicos. I wanted to tell the world just how much you mean to me."

"Oh, Xavier!" Porscha rushed toward him and jumped in his arms. He caught her and closed his mouth over hers. He deepened the kiss and their tongues dueled until they were both breathless and in need of oxygen.

Eventually, he slid Porscha back to her feet.

"I love you in ways I hadn't thought possible," Porscha said, holding both sides of his face as she looked up at him. "I love you with my heart, my body and my soul, Xavier. I thought I knew love before, but I was wrong. And I nearly ruined everything because I didn't cherish what we found. We have something special. Something one in a million."

"Yes. We do," Xavier said. "I think I knew it when we were at the clinic in Denver. I didn't want to admit my feelings for you then. You were still grappling with the media and I didn't want to hurt you, yet somehow I did."

"I had a trust issue after Gil," Porscha replied. "He made me doubt myself and my instincts. So I latched on to the first sign of trouble in our relationship because I was afraid. I had all these people from my mother to my record label whispering in my ear for so long. I couldn't hear my own voice, but I can now. I fired my mother."

"You did?"

Porscha nodded. "It had to be done. And guess what? It's been a turning point for us. I said things to her I should have said a long time ago, but once again I was too afraid to. But I don't want to live my life in fear. Not anymore. The sad, insecure woman you met in Denver is gone and in her place is a strong, powerful woman who is taking back her joy. I won't be afraid to feel. It's the best part of being alive."

Xavier leaned his forehead against hers. "Porscha, I'm so happy to see the change in you. The last couple of weeks have been hell without you. I wondered if I pushed you too hard to choose me. I would never want you to think you had to choose me over your career. I support you wholeheartedly. I just want to be by your side, loving you and being loved by you."

"Good, because I want to spend a lifetime with you,

Xavier," Porscha said, threading her arms around his waist. "I don't want to waste another second being apart."

"What are you saying?"

"Will you marry me, Xavier Lockett?" Porscha asked.

Xavier traced his fingertips down the side of her face and then cupped her chin. "Yes, I'll marry you." And with that, he scooped her legs right out from under her and began walking down the hall to the delight of the entire Lockett family standing there eavesdropping.

And once in the guesthouse, Xavier made sweet love to Porscha as she softly sang to him. That was when he told her, "You're my forever love."

Epilogue

The applause never ended.

"Can you hear that?" the TV announcer was saying into the camera. "That's Porscha Childs and her husband, Xavier Lockett, coming down the red carpet and they look amazing. Porscha is ravishing in an Oscar de la Renta Zac Posen gown while her husband is looking quite dapper in a Brioni Vanquish suit. Let's hope we can get them over."

A famous entertainment host motioned her and Xavier over to the dais and she gingerly made her way up the steps thanks to the help of her gracious husband. She was three months pregnant, so walking the red carpet in four-inch heels wasn't easy, but she was proud to attend the Oscars to celebrate her nomination for best original song, "Forever Love."

"Porscha, congratulations on the nomination," the host said. "Your first film and you win a Grammy and an Oscar nomination. That's no small feat."

"Thank you so much." Porscha beamed. "I'm so excited to be here. The film was a labor of love. I can't thank my costar Ryan Mills enough for helping this newbie find her voice."

"But that isn't your only news, is it?" the host inquired.

Porscha shook her head and turned to Xavier, who was grinning with pride at her side. "No, me and my husband are expecting our first child later this year." She patted her still flat stomach.

"Congratulations on both fronts," the host said with a thousand-watt smile.

Porscha waved at her fans and together she and Xavier left the dais to head inside the auditorium.

Hours later, she and Xavier were in a limousine heading to the Governors Ball.

"I can't believe it," Porscha said, looking down at the golden statute in her hands.

She'd just won her first Oscar for her original song on the film's soundtrack. She was on a high, but nothing could compete with having Xavier's love. They'd made it through life's ups and downs and come out stronger on the other side. Their wedding a few months ago had been small and quaint, much to Xavier's mother's chagrin, but Porscha figured Angelique had gotten the big wedding of her dreams with Giana and Wynn's five-hundred-guest blowout affair in Atlanta over the summer. And at the end of the day, Porscha had walked away with the best prize.

Xavier.

She glanced up into his dark gaze and found he was staring right back.

"What are you thinking about?" he asked, caressing her cheek.

"I'm thinking about how happy I am," Porscha said, "and how I can't wait to be a mother to our baby." She rolled her hand over the swell of her small stomach.

He sealed his lips over hers.

"What was that for?" she asked, looking up at him.

"For changing my world for the better."

* * * * *

Don't miss a single
Locketts of Tuxedo Park
story by Yahrah St. John!

Consequences of Passion
Blind Date with the Spare Heir
Holiday Playbook
A Game Between Friends

Available exclusively
from Harlequin Desire.

COMING NEXT MONTH FROM

DESIRE

#2881 ON OPPOSITE SIDES
Texas Cattleman's Club: Ranchers and Rivals
by Cat Schield
Determined to save her family ranch, Chelsea Grandin launches a daring scheme to seduce Nolan Thurston to discover his family's plans—and he does the same. Although they suspect they're using one another, their schemes disintegrate as attraction takes over...

#2882 ONE COLORADO NIGHT
Return to Catamount • by Joanne Rock
Cutting ties with her family, developer Jessamyn Barclay returns to the ranch to make peace, not expecting to see her ex, Ryder Wakefield. When one hot night changes everything, will they reconnect for their baby's sake or will a secret from the past ruin everything?

#2883 AFTER HOURS TEMPTATION
404 Sound • by Kianna Alexander
Focused on finishing an upcoming album, sound engineer Teagan Woodson and guitarist Maxton McCoy struggle to keep things professional as their attraction grows. But agreeing to "just a fling" may lead to *everything* around them falling apart...

#2884 WHEN THE LIGHTS GO OUT...
Angel's Share • by Jules Bennett
A blackout at her distillery leaves straitlaced Elise Hawthorne in the dark with her potential new client, restaurateur Antonio Rodriguez. One kiss leads to more, but everything is on the line when the lights come back on...

#2885 AN OFFER FROM MR. WRONG
Cress Brothers • by Niobia Bryant
Desperately needing a buffer between him and his newly discovered family, chef and reluctant heir Lincoln Cress turns to the one person who's all wrong for him—the PI who uncovered this information, Bobbie Barnett. But this fake relationship reveals very real desire...

#2886 HOW TO FAKE A WEDDING DATE
Little Black Book of Secrets • by Karen Booth
Infamous for canceling her million-dollar nuptials, Alexandra Gold is having a *little* trouble finding a date to the wedding of the season. Enter her brother's best friend, architect Ryder Carson. He's off-limits, so he's *safe*—except for the undeniable sparks between them!

Attorney Alexandra Lattimore isn't looking for love. She's home to help her family—and escape problems at work. But sparks with former rival Jackson Strom are too hot to resist. Will her secrets keep them from rewriting their past?

Read on for a sneak peek at
Rivalry at Play
by Nadine Gonzalez.

"Mornin'," Jackson said, as jovial at 6:00 a.m. as he was at noon. He loaded Alexa's bag into the trunk and held open the passenger door for her. "Let's get out of here."

Alexa hesitated. Within the blink of an eye, she'd slipped back in time. She was seventeen and Jackson was her prom date, holding open the door to a tacky rental limo. There he was, the object of her every teenage dream. She went over and touched him, just to make sure he was real.

"Are you okay?" he asked.

"No," she said. "I was thinking… If things were different back in high school—"

"Different how?"

"If I were nicer."

"Nicer?"

"Or just plain nice," she said. "Do you think you might have asked me to prom or homecoming or whatever?"

Jackson went still, but something moved in his eyes. Alexa panicked. What was she doing stirring things up at dawn?

"Forget it!" She backed away from him. "I don't know why I

said that. It's early and I haven't had coffee. Do you mind stopping for coffee along the way?"

He reached out and caught her by the waist. He pulled her close. The air between them was charged. "I didn't want *nice*. I wanted Alexandra Lattimore, the one girl who was anything but nice and who ran circles around me."

"Why didn't you say anything?"

"I was scared."

"You thought I'd reject you?"

"If I had asked you to prom or whatever, would you have said yes?"

"I don't know," she admitted. "Maybe not…or I could have changed my mind. Only it would have been too late. You would have found yourself a less complicated date."

"And end up having a forgettable night?"

"That's not so bad," she said. "I would have ended up hating myself."

Alexa wanted to be that person he'd imagined, imperious and unimpressed by her peers or her surroundings, but she wasn't. She never had been. She'd lived her whole life in a self-protective mode, rejecting others before they could reject or dismiss her. She now saw it for what it was: a coward's device.

His hand fell from her waist. He stepped back and held open the car door even wider. "Aren't you happy we're not those foolish kids anymore?"

Alexa leaned forward and kissed him lightly on the lips. "You have no idea," she whispered and slid into the waiting seat.

Don't miss what happens next in…
Rivalry at Play *by Nadine Gonzalez,*
the next book in the Texas Cattleman's Club:
Ranchers and Rivals *series!*

Available July 2022 wherever
Harlequin Desire *books and ebooks are sold.*

Harlequin.com

Get 4 FREE REWARDS!

We'll send you 2 FREE Books plus 2 FREE Mystery Gifts.

FREE Value Over **$20**

Both the **Harlequin® Desire** and **Harlequin Presents®** series feature compelling novels filled with passion, sensuality and intriguing scandals.

YES! Please send me 2 FREE novels from the Harlequin Desire or Harlequin Presents series and my 2 FREE gifts (gifts are worth about $10 retail). After receiving them, if I don't wish to receive any more books, I can return the shipping statement marked "cancel." If I don't cancel, I will receive 6 brand-new Harlequin Presents Larger-Print books every month and be billed just $5.80 each in the U.S. or $5.99 each in Canada, a savings of at least 11% off the cover price or 6 Harlequin Desire books every month and be billed just $4.55 each in the U.S. or $5.24 each in Canada, a savings of at least 13% off the cover price. It's quite a bargain! Shipping and handling is just 50¢ per book in the U.S. and $1.25 per book in Canada.* I understand that accepting the 2 free books and gifts places me under no obligation to buy anything. I can always return a shipment and cancel at any time. The free books and gifts are mine to keep no matter what I decide.

Choose one: ☐ **Harlequin Desire**
(225/326 HDN GNND)

☐ **Harlequin Presents Larger-Print**
(176/376 HDN GNWY)

Name (please print)

Address   Apt. #

City   State/Province   Zip/Postal Code

Email: Please check this box ☐ if you would like to receive newsletters and promotional emails from Harlequin Enterprises ULC and its affiliates. You can unsubscribe anytime.

Mail to the **Harlequin Reader Service:**
IN U.S.A.: P.O. Box 1341, Buffalo, NY 14240-8531
IN CANADA: P.O. Box 603, Fort Erie, Ontario L2A 5X3

Want to try 2 free books from another series! Call 1-800-873-8635 or visit www.ReaderService.com.

*Terms and prices subject to change without notice. Prices do not include sales taxes, which will be charged (if applicable) based on your state or country of residence. Canadian residents will be charged applicable taxes. Offer not valid in Quebec. This offer is limited to one order per household. Books received may not be as shown. Not valid for current subscribers to the Harlequin Presents or Harlequin Desire series. All orders subject to approval. Credit or debit balances in a customer's account(s) may be offset by any other outstanding balance owed by or to the customer. Please allow 4 to 6 weeks for delivery. Offer available while quantities last.

Your Privacy—Your information is being collected by Harlequin Enterprises ULC, operating as Harlequin Reader Service. For a complete summary of the information we collect, how we use this information and to whom it is disclosed, please visit our privacy notice located at corporate.harlequin.com/privacy-notice. From time to time we may also exchange your personal information with reputable third parties. If you wish to opt out of this sharing of your personal information, please visit readerservice.com/consumerschoice or call 1-800-873-8635. **Notice to California Residents**—Under California law, you have specific rights to control and access your data. For more information on these rights and how to exercise them, visit corporate.harlequin.com/california-privacy.

HDHP22

HQN

Welcome to Four Corners Ranch, Maisey Yates's newest miniseries, where the West is still wild...and when a cowboy needs a wife, he decides to find her the old-fashioned way!

Evelyn Moore can't believe she's agreed to uproot her city life to become Oregon cowboy and single dad Sawyer Garrett's mail-order bride. Her love for his tiny daughter is instant. Her feelings for Sawyer are...more complicated. Her gruff cowboy husband ignites a thrilling desire in her, but Sawyer is determined to keep their marriage all about the baby. But what happens if Evelyn wants it all?

The front door opened, and a man came out. He had on a black cowboy hat, and he was holding a baby. Those were the first two details she took in, but then there was… Well, there was the whole rest of him.

Evelyn could feel his eyes on her from some fifty feet away, could see the piercing blue color. His nose was straight and strong, as was his jaw. His lips were remarkable, and she didn't think she had ever really found lips on a man all that remarkable. He had the sort of symmetrical good looks that might make a man almost too pretty, but he was saved from that by a scar that edged through the corner of his mouth, creating a thick white line that disrupted the symmetry there. He was tall. Well over six feet, and broad.

And his arms were…

Good Lord.

He was wearing a short-sleeved black T-shirt, and he cradled the tiny baby in the crook of a massive bicep and forearm. He could easily lift bales of hay and throw them around. Hell, he could probably easily lift the truck and throw it around.

He was beautiful. Objectively, absolutely beautiful.

But there was something more than that. Because as he walked toward her, she felt like he was stealing increments of her breath, emptying her lungs. She'd seen handsome men before. She'd been around celebrities who were touted as the sexiest men on the planet.

But she had never felt anything quite like this.

Because this wasn't just about how he looked on the outside, though it was sheer masculine perfection; it was about what he did to her insides. Like he had taken the blood in her veins and replaced it with fire. And she could say with absolute honesty she had never once in all of her days wanted to grab a stranger and fling herself at him, and push them both into the nearest closet, bedroom, whatever, and…

Well, everything.

But she felt it, right then and there with him.

And there was something about the banked heat in his blue eyes that made her think he might feel exactly the same way.

And suddenly she was terrified of all the freedom. Giddy with it, which went right along with that joy/terror paradox from before.

She didn't know anyone here. She had come without anyone's permission or approval. She was just here. With this man. And there was nothing to stop them from…anything.

Except he was holding a baby and his sister was standing right to her left. But otherwise…

She really hoped that he was Sawyer. Because if he was Wolf, it was going to be awkward.

"Evelyn," he said. And goose bumps broke out over her arms. And she knew. Because he was the same man who had told her that she would be making him meat loaf whether she liked it or not.

And suddenly the reason it had felt distinctly sexual this time became clear.

"Yes," she responded.

"Sawyer," he said. "Sawyer Garrett." And then he absurdly took a step forward and held his hand out. To shake. And she was going to have to… touch him. Touch him and not melt into a puddle at his feet.

Find out what happens next in Evelyn and Sawyer's marriage deal in Unbridled Cowboy, *the unmissable first installment in Maisey Yates's new Four Corners Ranch miniseries.*

Don't miss Unbridled Cowboy *by New York Times bestselling author Maisey Yates, available May 2022 wherever HQN books and ebooks are sold.*

HQNBooks.com